KNIGHT

OF

Bronzeville

Book 2 of the Knights of the Castle Series

Naleighna Kai
Stephanie M. Freeman

Macro Publishing Group
Chicago, Illinois

This is a work of fiction. Names, characters, places, and incidents are products of the author's imagination or are used fictitiously and are not to be construed as real. Any resemblance to actual events, locales, organizations, or persons, living or dead, is entirely coincidental.

Knight of Bronzeville by Naleighna Kai and Stephanie M. Freeman
Copyright ©2020
ISBN: [Ebook] 978-1-952871-01-6
ISBN: [Trade Paperback] 978-1-952871-09-2

Macro Publishing Group
1507 E. 53rd Street, #858
Chicago, IL 60615

All rights reserved. No part of this book may be used or reproduced in any manner whatsoever or by any means including electronic, mechanical or photocopying, or stored in a retrieval system without written permission of the author, except in the case of brief quotations embodied in critical articles and reviews. For permission, contact Naleighna Kai at naleighnakai@gmail.com or at www.naleighnakai.com

Cover Designed by: J.L Woodson: www.woodsoncreativestudio.com
Interior Designed by: Lissa Woodson: www.naleighnakai.com
Editors: J. L. Campbell jlcampbellwrites@gmail.com;
Betas: Debra J. Mitchell, Ellen Kiley Goeckler, Brynn Weimer, April Bubb, and Kelsie Maxwell

KNIGHT OF Bronzeville

Book 2 of the Knights of the Castle Series

Naleighna Kai and Stephanie M. Freeman

♦ DEDICATION ♦

Naleighna Kai's Dedication:

Jean Woodson, Eric Harold Spears, LaKecia Janise Woodson, Mildred E. Williams, Anthony Johnson,
L. A. Banks, Octavia Butler, Tanishia Pearson Jones, Emmanuel McDavid, and Priscilla Jackson.
To Robert Walker, the love of Pat G'Orge-Walker's life. Through her stories about you, I have come to understand the kind of love that transcends time, distance, and lifetimes.

Stephanie M. Freeman's Dedication:

For Dolores Ann Wilkes, my Mother, my friend, my first editor. When I gave you my first page, you said, "That's nice, but I want to hear 'your voice'. You're your story, your way. Promise me that you will."
This started my writing journey. Mama, I kept my word.

♦ ACKNOWLEDGEMENTS ♦

First and foremost, all praises due to the Creator for excellent health and strength, for peace of mind and prosperity; for all things great and small.

Special thanks to the Creator from whom all blessings flow, many thanks goes out to: Sesvalah, J. L. Woodson (my Number One Son!), Jennifer Cole Addison (author J. S. Cole, my number one niece!), Stephanie M. Freeman (thanks for jumping in at the 11th hour to make this book shine), Debra J. Mitchell, J. L. Campbell, Kelly Peterson, Janine A. Ingram, Ehryck F. Gilmore, Kelsie Maxwell, LaVerne Thomspon, Kassanna Dwight, Vikkas Bhardwaj, Ella Houston, Amanda McCoy, Ellen Kiley Goeckler, Siera London, J. D. Mason, Brynn Weimer, April Bubb, Marie J. Robinson, Elizabeth Means, Frankie Payne, the Kings of the Castle Ambassadors, Members of Naleighna Kai's Literary Cafe, the members of NK Tribe Called Success, the members of Namakir Tribe, and to you, my dear readers . . . thank you all for your support.

Much love, peace, abundance, and joy,

Naleighna Kai

STEPHANIE M. FREEMAN

Naleighna Kai thank you for finding this 'Wordsmith' and making me part of the tribe. J.L Woodson for such marvelous Graphic Designer eyes. Debra J. Mitchell, Brynn Weimer, and Ellen Kiley, April Bubb for your feedback. Namakir Tribe and NK's Tribe Called Success for their never-ending support. To my family, thanks for being here. To readers who have traveled this journey with me from thrillers to erotica, and now romantic suspense—thank you!

Happy reading,

Stephanie M. Freeman

Chapter 1

Two officers marched toward Mandy, determination in every stride as their feet padded against the carpeted floors of Sangster International Airport. Despite the warm weather of Jamaica, a shiver of alarm went up her spine. She wasn't sure why.

"Ms. McCoy," the taller of the two said. "Come wit' us."

Her heart thumped hard and breathing became labored. "What's going on?"

"We understand that ya made a complaint last night? Need ta ask ya some tings."

Mandy took a calming breath, left her chair at the airport gate, then followed them through the airport maze. Along the way, she tried to tamp down on the anger she had every right to feel. She hoped this would not be a part of another ugly experience on this vacation. One that she had sacrificed a great deal—personally and financially—to accomplish.

Making matters worse, they weren't talking—at least to her. They muttered code words to one another on the walkie talkies attached to their shoulders, but never to her.

"Can you tell me what this is about or at least where we are going?"

The taller of the two gestured to a point behind him. "Right dis way, madam."

Those words were spoken in that lyrical musical accent she loved on the regular, but each time they said the words now, her belly swam further south. She tried to match their much longer, more purposeful strides.

Crowds of travelers gave them a wide berth as they continued to make their way to wherever 'dis way' happened to be. They rounded several long walkways before reaching a series of corridors that led further and further away from the hustle and bustle of other travelers and the announcements piped through the terminal. All the while, her mind raced as she attempted to pinpoint where things had gone left.

Her mind filtered through many things, but settled on the scene outside the terminal aiming to make it to her Chicago flight, when a brunette had been shoved into the back of a limousine. The man, wearing a distinctive designer suit with a red ascot, and a pirate-worthy eye patch, finally put his focus back on the woman who laughed before he did one last sweep of the area. Then his gaze settled on Mandy's face as though to memorize her, but his one available eye widened with shock. The woman was laughing as well. Or could it have been mistaken for sobbing? The airbrakes on the shuttle pulling into the parking area drowned out most virtually everything else.

Mandy was still trying to place where she remembered him from when that same man nearly knocked her down as he sprinted through the revolving doors towards security. The dirty look he'd given her as he mouthed some hateful, hurtful thing made her glad she couldn't hear him clearly.

Everything was a jumble from day one of landing on the island until last night. She remembered taking a trip from her adjoining bedroom suite to the kitchen and found that the balcony door was open. Soon the bed squeaking, grunts, and groans from the room below hers was followed by a late-night argument. Shortly thereafter, in a sleep-filled haze, Mandy vaguely heard the sound of a balloon popping and then a welcomed silence followed.

Her one and only call to the front desk was met with a raspy voice promising to check on that strange noise, but didn't receive a return call to say the matter had been resolved. As she left that morning, she noticed that the desk attendants were staring aguardt her as if she'd stolen something when she retuned her keys.

The drops of what looked like coffee on the white doorframe filtered into her mind. Blood. She was sure of it. She'd seen her share of detective shows and while she was no expert, she'd seen the episode that talked about blood spray patterns and cast off.

No, something did happen. So, it wasn't a dream. No balloons breaking, that sound was gun fire. Hadn't they said on one show that suppressors could be made out of just about anything? Clothing, Soda bottles. Forget the idea of using a pillow. Even housekeeping would have picked up on the missing pillow or the blood. Unless, of course, it had been an inside job.

Mandy tried to shake off the dread winding through her muscles as she tried to keep up with the officers.

Get a grip Mandy. You're getting paranoid. This is all some misunderstanding. All they will do is take a statement. It wasn't like you went down to the room and banged on the door. Some huge mistake. Has to be. Last thing you need is to get noticed by law enforcement. Calm down.

What else could go wrong? Even the workshop and medical consultation, the main purpose of her trip, had hit its own snag; one that almost sent her tearing off to be on the first flight home.

Now this.

One of the officers, a man with a dark complexion and close-cropped haircut, kept glancing over his shoulder to see if she was keeping in step with them. Wasn't like she could take off running in any direction with the crowd around them. Her plane was set to leave in two hours and security had snatched her up before she could inform anyone in her family of these unfolding developments.

Technically, she wasn't supposed to be off American soil. She had taken a risk, because despite the restitution center's restrictions, her passport was still in her possession. She would pay the outrageous court fees they had demanded when she returned.

The officers escorted her into a room with gray walls, a scarred wooden table, metal chairs, and a wall clock as the only décor. One of them pointed to a seat, and she complied.

At this point, the shorter of the male officers left and a uniformed female stepped inside. Her locs were pulled into a ponytail and her cold eyes sized up Mandy.

"Why were ya here on my island?" the man with a beautiful dark complexion asked.

"I came for a consultation and a workshop," she answered, adjusting the pashmina around her shoulders.

"Do ya have any proof?"

Mandy sighed, reached into her tote, pulled out her cell, and scrolled to the few pictures that detailed her stay. She had come seeking a consult, an alternative to the cocktail of medications prescribed by her American doctors that she refused to take, but found a spiritual awakening instead.

The nightmares that stemmed from a horrific experience had returned with a vengeance. She saw no need to be medicated to deal with such a thing. Something had to exist that would help her get a handle on the reasons she couldn't leave that incident with those guards in Mississippi in the shadows.

At first, the conference had been long on promise but fell short on delivery. Until the co-host, Chaz Maharaj, had taken her for private sessions after she'd been humiliated by Susan Keller, the main host.

The officers continued to ask her a myriad of questions, some of them strange, because none of them mattered in the scheme of things. Was she alone or was she with someone? What was her destination? Why was she petrified around the canine units?

What the hell is really going on? Canine units. She was terrified of dogs! The night that she managed to escape those guards, they had them searching for her everywhere. The barking was endless. Just the look or sound of them could strike fear in her heart and take her back to that ill-fated time. Why wouldn't she be nervous with guards in full tactical gear marching around with them? Who wouldn't be?

"But ya heard som'ting in da room below yours?"

"Yes, I did, and I called the front desk. No one called back to say anything. There were loud voices and a little screaming, so I figured it was a simple domestic dispute. It quieted down after I made the call and I was able to get some sleep."

The officers exchanged a worried glance. "And that is when you heard a gunshot? What kind of gun was it?"

"No clue, like I said. It sounded like a balloon popping." She shifted in the chair and sighed. "Did someone go and do a welfare check? I mean what is this? Did you find a body or something? Look, just tell me what the hell is going on."

The officers looked at one another yet again, then back at her before excusing themselves.

After another fifteen minutes, they returned with another man dressed in a suit.

"You know what," she said as she stood and gathered her things. "Unless you're going to tell me why you brought me here, or do you plan on purchasing another set of tickets for me..." She shrugged, despite her rising level of annoyance.

The male officer stood to his full height. "What do you think we found in the room below yours?"

She gave that a moment's thought. "Okay, so maybe I just imagined the whole thing."

The burly man in the suit stepped forward as he reached into his coat and pulled out a detective's shield. Mandy's legs nearly buckled.

"But also in your room…"

Mandy barely noticed that he, unlike the officers, spoke full on English, but his last words were alarming. "What about it?"

"Well, the doorknob and door frame tested positive for blood. Did you happen to cut yourself before you left the …" The detective eyed the Band-Aid glued to the palm of her hand.

Mandy lifted her hand, the memory of how she acquired it kicked in. Why would that be of concern to them? "I broke a juice glass this morning. That's all."

The three men and lone woman in the room were silent so long, a sinking feeling settled in the pit of her belly.

"I think you better have a seat, Ms. McCoy," he said, his tone grave and chilling. "Will you submit to a search and a blood test, just for *exclusion* purposes?"

Mandy flinched as he rounded the table and came toward her. "Are you serious?"

His serious expression matched his words. "Yes, unless you have something to hide. You won't let the dogs near you, so we'll have to take your belongings to them."

They were treating her like a criminal when all she came to do was find answers in a warm, exotic place.

"This cannot be happening," she whispered, shooting a panicked glance at the female officer. "Fine. And I don't want a man to do it," Mandy insisted, putting the male officer on notice. Why they wouldn't consider that an issue mystified her.

Even still, she had to be careful with how she handled things. She couldn't make waves because the fact that she had been out of the country might make it back to the wrong people. Then her freedom could be snatched at any time.

She stood the moment a second female officer arrived. With a glance at the male to nudge him to leave, the two women took their own sweet time doing the search as seconds ticked away. Some areas they touched twice, almost as if trying to verify a breast was a breast, a thigh was a thigh. Then they drew bloodwork before making her strip to the bone and carted her clothing and tote bag out to wherever they kept those dogs.

The chill of the room made her tremble, but she was more afraid of other things she hadn't considered. One, her nephew Christian, and her niece, Blair, didn't know she was being held up on this end. Two, they had taken her phone an hour ago and it hadn't been returned, so she couldn't call her family. Three, she had already explained to them several times over that she made no detours or pit stops of any kind. She even went so far as to check her bags before she made a mad dash to the bathroom to relieve herself.

Something about this whole scenario felt wrong, but protesting could put her in even more hot water if she didn't get back to Chicago and make good on her responsibilities. She was barely on the right side of freedom as it was. "I'm going to miss my flight."

"So ya miss it," the loc-wearing woman snapped, her dark eyes boring into Mandy's.

Mandy prayed for patience. "There are no other non-stops back to the States until tomorrow."

The second woman with a washed-out complexion, shrugged. "Put your tings back on."

It took everything inside Mandy to keep from diving off the deep end and taking an ugly swim. "May I make a phone call?" she asked as she hurriedly dressed, checking the wall clock once again, which caused panic to set in.

"No calls here."

"I need to contact my family to let them know where I am," Mandy said, hating the desperate edge to her voice.

"If ya can finda way …" The woman tilted her head, and Mandy could swear she smirked.

When the sullen officer handed Mandy the cell, she tried to get a signal while they walked her halfway across the airport, but none of her texts or emails went through after several attempts.

Finally, after she hurriedly made arrangements with another airline, one of the women escorted Mandy through customs, and she was on a plane. Not the original non-stop flight, but an aircraft bound for Mississippi, then to Chicago, nonetheless. She glanced at the courtesy luggage tear off claims in her hands and teared up a little. *Great, my bags will probably make it home or to West Hell before I do. That is, if they even made it on the first plane. Damn, that one blouse ... the one Chaz said made me look like a beautiful butterfly ... that line was corny as hell, but the way he said it, though.* She believed him, and now the blouse—and him—were nothing more than a distant memory. At least she had those to hold on to.

She closed her eyes, said a prayer of thanks, settled into the seat, and prepared for the plane to push back from the gate.

Mandy felt them before she saw them. The airport officers appeared at the moment an overhead announcement blared, "Amanda McCoy, you are wanted in security."

Again? Mandy tried to hold back tears of frustration and barely succeeded. She unlocked the seatbelt and followed the two familiar women off the plane and back to that sparse little room she'd been in for nearly two hours.

And now, for another round of mindless questioning. The fear that she would never see home again set in. She couldn't get reception on the way to the plane, so she still hadn't reached anyone in the States. And the officers took her phone again. No one knew she was still on the island and not headed for a new flight home, now with a connection in Mississippi, except these burly, sour-faced women who seemed determined to keep Mandy in Jamaica far longer than she ever intended.

"So, I'm going to have to catch yet another flight, huh?" she asked, after answering the same questions she'd already cleared before.

"Oh, ya got bigger problems," the officer with reddish-brown hair warned.

Mandy inhaled and let out that breath slowly, but her heart hammered against her chest—an all too familiar occurrence over the past three hours.

"Da last connecting one leaves in five minutes, but we have more questions."

That meant she would be stuck in Jamaica all night with these two new Keystone cops riding her ass.

Chapter 2

"This marriage has been based on a lie from day one," Chaz said, trying to keep his anger in check. "You knew what I desired, but you dragged things out until it became an absolute impossibility. You were well aware that being honest would have saved both of us a great deal of anguish and time."

Susan shrank back and pushed the strands of hair away from her face, tucking them behind her ears. Pain flared in all areas of her heart. He was right. She had never, *ever* wanted children and thought she'd navigated the issue well. First, Chaz mentioned having a big family. Five years later, the request became four children. Five years after that, the request was for two. Then finally, when he approached forty, he pleaded for one. *Just one*.

No, she wouldn't tell him about the three children she almost had. She went through with the procedures, then had her best friend and assistant, Morgan, schedule a retreat away from him, giving her time to recover. Chaz had been none the wiser.

Why bring children into such an ugly world? So many were already unloved and uncared for. The world couldn't take care of its own life forces, let alone new ones brought in.

Lately, even when dealing with business ventures, he'd become more distant, preferring to go through their attorneys instead. Though she'd been paying the judge under the table to keep the divorce on ice for as long as he could, the reconciliation efforts the judge insisted on had all been for naught. She couldn't remember the last time Chaz had touched her sexually, even before he initiated the divorce. And the man was voracious when it came to all appetites.

She had even thrown out a "hall pass" suggestion to give him the option to seek a little sexual satisfaction, but even that didn't seem to faze him. The divorce was so close to final—even with every stalling tactic her lawyer and the judge could secretly manage—but because their business endeavors and real estate interests were tightly woven, they had settled into a life restrained by an outward show of togetherness. Internally, he was kind, respectful even, but ... drifting.

"I am sorry that I hurt you," she whispered, reaching for him. He instantly pulled away and she had to wonder what had really transpired during those private sessions with Amanda McCoy.

As an international figure, women were attracted not only to his wickedly handsome good looks, but the charisma and vivaciousness that was so much a part of who he was. Chaz was totally unaware of his effect on women and men alike. People gravitated to his peaceful and confident nature. She had wanted him the first time she laid eyes on him at an Earth Day Convention and Music Festival in London.

A conversation turned into dinner, dinner turned into friendship, friendship turned into a proposal that shocked the entire world. Susan Keller, medical maven, marrying Chaz Maharaj, the spokesperson for a major pharmaceutical company, became big news in Europe, India, England, and America. She basked in the jealousy from women who wondered what she, a woman from America's South, had done to land the most handsome man in the world. One whose career took off in a totally different direction after that first commercial. She had him all to herself and didn't want to share. Especially with something as demanding as a child.

Susan had worked ages to perfect her figure—no surgery, just hard work and determined flexibility. A child would have destroyed those efforts. Then when Chaz threw out the idea of adoption, she cringed and replied with that yammer about wanting children of their bloodlines. Years later, surrogacy became a thing and he tossed that idea into the marriage pot. She rejected every single one of the women he personally selected. Thankfully, he finally gave up.

Right at the point she believed she was totally in the clear, he brought it up again and she finally told him she was too old to go through all the procedures it would take to bear a child. That whole egg extraction thing sounded painful. She was having none of that.

Only then did he accept full-on reality that she had lied about her intentions all along.

This unfortunate incident at their latest full retreat was reflective of the current state of affairs. Total disconnect and chaos.

The whole retreat concept had been a bone of contention between them from the very start. This yoga, chanting, meditation-filled holistic hogwash was not the kind of work Susan had envisioned when she finished medical school at the top of her class, or when she founded her own multi-million-dollar practice after residency. Chaz, however, leaned more toward Eastern spirituality than Western medicine and had found peace and guidance for himself through these practices.

Now that he sought to end things between them romantically, he was adamant about going full out in this direction—combining fitness, nutrition, meditation, and other techniques for health and wellness. A bunch of new aged mumbo-jumbo in her book. Tried and true scientific methods worked best. What good was all the lab work, the controlled research trials, the pharmaceutical companies, if people were going to disregard what the experts and medical professionals had to say?

So when the American woman, Amanda McCoy, called and asked if the event had classes and information tailored to women of a certain size, Susan was taken aback. The woman said *plus*, but she should've been honest and said *fat*. Anything over a size six was suspect, and Mandy had to be a cool fourteen-sixteen. No, Susan had already made enough concessions with Chaz going all "faith, hope, and love" when it came to healing practices, derailing all of their hard-built medical practices. No, they weren't going to make allowances for people who had no self-control and were out of shape. Unfortunately, what Susan said was "Yes, we will have a special class strictly for plus-size women for basic consultations and things of that nature."

The lie slipped off her tongue so fast, but Susan didn't think anything more about it because those kinds of people rarely had any real interest in her classes. The videos and photos they had taken during the last workshop in St. Martinique reflected who was *actually* welcome. So, shock set in when she realized Amanda had actually traveled to Jamaica. The woman stepped into the room, surveyed the area for a few moments, taking in the fact that every single person was in shape—mostly a room of wealthy white women in size zero lululemon gear. She inched backward, preparing to leave.

Susan couldn't have cared less one way or another since the fees were non-refundable. She could use every dime right now. After another medical malpractice suit that she managed to keep hidden from Chaz; she was paying increased insurance amounts and fines up the wazoo and barely holding onto her medical license. So Mandy's going or staying was no skin off her nose.

Then Chaz lost his mind when he called out, asking, "Wait, why are you leaving?"

The woman seemed to fold in on herself when all eyes turned her way. A few snickers and conversations ensued.

"I'm in the wrong place."

"Did you register for Holistic Healing Methods?" Chaz asked, leaving Susan's side and weaving through the guests, bare feet padding against the wood floor.

"Yes, and a few other workshops, but I was told this part of it was—"

"You were told what?" Susan snapped, trying to make sure the plump female did not tip her hand. "This is open to everyone."

The woman's dark brown eyes widened in shock, raven curls bounced the moment her head tilted. "That's not—"

Squaring her shoulders, Susan said, "Why do you people always expect —"

Unfortunately, in her anger, she had ignored the cringes and grimaces from some of the women in the room. Four of them gathered their belongings and prepared to leave.

Chaz whirled to face Susan and said, "What is wrong with you? Do you know how that sounds? Apologize now."

Susan flinched, but regrouped enough to lift her chin. "She knows what I meant."

"And that's the problem. She does and is highly offended." He tilted his head, peering at her. "For you to allow something so vile to leave your mouth means I never knew you."

Susan folded her arms across her bosom, trying to contain her alarm at the disagreement taking place in front of people, professionals in their field along with members of their families who had worked with them for years. Here, the second time they were executing this "newfound" direction Chaz demanded they travel in. They were arguing instead of presenting a united front as they had always done—the medical world's dynamic duo. "We will discuss this at a later time."

"You will apologize right now," he said through his teeth, and a few others near him nodded.

"Oh, there's trouble in paradise, huh?" one of the guests whispered loud enough for Susan to hear.

She lasered in on the woman who made that comment. The blonde turned and the woman next to her shifted until a few inches of space opened between them.

"What led you to believe this class was specifically designed for a particular group of people?" Chaz asked.

"Fat people," Susan corrected, loud enough to carry the length of the room. Several heads snapped to her.

Chaz shot her a look that would have withered another person on the spot before focusing on the stranger. "She is not fat; she's curvaceous." His gaze swept across Susan and flickered to Mandy before he said, "You know, someone who happens to be more meat than bone. Some men appreciate that—a full meal, rather than an appetizer. I most certainly do." He didn't give Susan a chance to respond before his gaze locked in on the stranger and said, "And your name is ... "

"Amanda McCoy, but call me Mandy," she replied, blinking back a little confusion probably caused by the huskiness of his voice when he made that damning statement about Susan's rail thin size compared to Mandy's medium height and curves that had the men in the room giving her a second and third look. She quickly took her focus away from Susan, pulled out her phone to filter through her emails, then turned it to face Chaz.

Susan wanted to interrupt, take control of the unsettled class by asking him to remove the woman from the room. Curiosity won out. She left her spot in the front and made it to where Chaz and the interloper stood. She wanted to hear exactly what "Mandy" told Chaz.

Scanning the screen, his expression went from shocked, to resigned, then thunderous.

"Oh, so she came with receipts?" Susan taunted with a shrug.

"I don't bring receipts," Mandy shot back, turning the phone so it faced Susan full on. "I brought invoices. And you lied."

"And it's not the first time," Chaz whispered. "Our entire marriage started on a lie and it's ending that way."

Several gasps echoed, then more people stood and gathered their things.

Fury gripped Susan and she flicked a wrist toward Mandy. "You care more about some stranger that you would put such a blatant statement out there? How dare you."

"Come," he said beckoning to Mandy. "You came all this way for her class and consultation. I will give you a private one."

"I would like to come, too," another patron whined. Others joined in with the same request.

"I hear you," Susan said, "It's not going to be so peaceful with all of this negative vibe up in here."

Chaz extended his hand to Mandy, but turned to address their guests. "You paid to see Susan, and I won't take away her students. I was merely here to support and assist with this part of things—but I have plans underway to execute my own business. This woman, Mandy, traveled all this way for something that does not exist. I think it is only fair that she is adequately compensated for her time." He reached for the tote bag Mandy was carrying and said, "Follow me."

The moment Mandy's hand touched his, something sparked between them and they both pulled away. Susan saw it too, but brushed it off. She leaned in so only the two of them could hear. "Remember that hall pass I said you could have?"

Chaz glared, nearly singeing her with those piercing dark-brown eyes.

"That's the woman I'd pick for you."

Susan turned her back to him and walked away with a laugh she hoped would chill him all the way to the bone.

Evidently, it had," she mused, giving Chaz a onceover. "The wrong bone, though. Definitely the wrong bone.

Chapter 3

"Can I go now?" Mandy asked, weary of the humiliation of being detained and searched by security. First that business at the resort, being on display and called out because of her physical appearance, but now this. The second time in her life she'd ever been popular, and lo and behold, it was for the wrong thing, again.

Even as a child she was used to the incredulous looks or the barely covered laughs or whispers as she walked by, but this was ten-times worse. Not only was she under a microscope, but they weren't even giving her straight answers.

She'd endured the laughter or the snide remarks all of her life, but to ask a question and be ignored or patronized as if somehow something about her denoted a lack of intelligence, made her blood boil. Speaking up or speaking out was a mistake, because then she ended up being labeled as difficult or suffering from an acute case of Angry Woman Syndrome. Women were supposed to be friendly and agreeable to a fault, and any other response could be considered an imposition or blatant rudeness.

Never mind the inconvenience to her at this point in time. She was expected to be humble and gracious no matter what the cost to her, personally. She already knew the song, but this verse, right here and right now, was totally new. She didn't know what lessons she was supposed to derive from this experience, but it was major.

The grumpy woman nodded. "Ya can head out t'morrow."

Mandy wanted to sink to the floor. By now her suitcases, and all the precious things that Chaz had purchased for her while on the island, were circling somewhere—without her. Hopefully, they'd meet somewhere when she made it home to Chicago. The only thing she had was the tote, her identification, some cash, and an electronic tablet.

Mandy pulled out her phone that had just enough charge and finally a signal to make a call to the States. She phoned Christian, who nearly used up the rest of her available charge by throwing a world of unnecessary questions her way. Finally, she cut through his chatter and snapped, "Christian, please call the resort and see if they can have someone come get me."

"But—"

"Do it," she shot back. "I don't have much time."

Mandy refused to cry. All she wanted to do was go home and couldn't figure how customs had singled her out for this type of treatment.

She made it inside the resort and to the front desk. Sondra, a woman she recognized from earlier in the week, greeted her warmly this time. "Weren't you supposed to leave t'day?"

"Yes, but I'm back and need a room for the night."

Sondra peered at her and the smile disappeared as she keyed in some information into the computer, then said, "Five hundred dollars. And we want cash."

Mandy inhaled and the blood rushed to her head. She stilled her mind, pulled out her phone and typed in some information of her own.

Then she turned the screen toward the desk clerk and said, "Where's Lynae?"

At the mention of the co-worker who had helped Chaz Maharaj secure better accommodations for Mandy on her first day in Jamaica, Sondra's face was nowhere near as friendly as it had been as she stared at Mandy with cold eyes. "She gone home."

With her back ramrod straight, Mandy said, "I'd like to speak with your manager, please."

Sondra trudged away, glanced over her shoulder at Mandy a moment, then disappeared in the back office. She returned with a tall, dark, well-built man, who scanned the screen and peered at her before he asked, "What's your name?"

"Amanda McCoy."

"Ah, yes," he said. "Christian Vidal called ahead. He's already rented an upper floor suite and paid for the night, plus dinner and breakfast."

Mandy had never been so grateful in her life. Her nephew had earned major points for that one. That's why she loved him and Blair so much. Her niece and nephew always had her back.

Even when the resort offered to send up room service, she was so distraught that eating was the last thing on her mind.

Chaz Maharaj had taken up residence in her thoughts instead. He had those dark brown orbs that caused her to melt in all the places that counted; that smooth olive complexion her fingers longed to stroke; those lips curved in such a sensuous way that she still felt some kind of heat just thinking about them. The last three hours were swept away as he settled into her memories for the night and thoughts of him finally put her in the mind to have sweet dreams.

* * *

Chaz was stretched out in the master bedroom of the presidential suite, angry that once again Susan had caused everyone a world of trouble. Now they were here in Jamaica for one more night. Susan had it so far in for Mandy that she shot off her mouth and the bullet landed in her own foot and his, too.

They should have been on a flight to Mississippi for the next retreat given in Susan's hometown. The location had been his suggestion because if they could get the ultra-conservative people she had grown up with on board, then maybe she'd stop giving him such a hard time about the direction he'd always wanted to move in. Finally, as part of the concessions, she had insisted that all of these new aspects run through her company and that she would be the face of this part of their business ventures. He had agreed for the first three of the trial run—Martinique, Jamaica, and then Mississippi before putting together a plan to add any others. She still felt her current market should be the target. Chaz felt differently, knowing that expanding beyond the wealthy demographic was the way to go.

He did a quick search for his private journal and came up empty. After nearly thirty minutes, he gave up, but hoped that it wasn't in Susan's possession. So many private thoughts after his sessions with Mandy had been placed between the pages. He took another sip of the wine that Mandy favored and smiled. Chaz wasn't a sweet libation kind of man, but it was growing on him, and so had Mandy. The dark silky curls that bounced with every move; the honey skin just pleading for him to press a kiss to its warmth. Those eyes—they slayed him. Such pain they held that made him wonder what had happened in her life to bring her to that point. He had made the right choice in removing himself from Susan on day one, which would set the stage for how the rest of this new venture would go.

Chaz guided Mandy to the front desk, where a woman with locs touching her shoulder greeted them with a bright smile. Her cheerful attitude contrasted with Mandy's trembling form. Her anger over Susan's treatment had not dissipated.

Guests wandered through the lobby area and another couple stood at the counter, dealing with a member of staff.

"My name's Sondra. How may I help you?" The front desk clerk narrowed her gaze on Mandy before focusing on Chaz once again and giving him an appreciative look that didn't mirror the disapproving one she had given Mandy.

"I'd like to have a separate suite for the rest of this week. The presidential suite, please."

"But weren't you rooming with—"

"I'd like my own place for the rest of my stay here."

Sondra blinked twice, tapped on the keyboard and pulled up the roster of available rooms. "The resort is full. Overbooked, in fact."

"Right," he said. "I'm almost positive there is something on the upper floors that is available."

"Oh, the suites?" Her gaze turned more assessing. "Those are for special guests."

"How special?"

Her gaze flickered to Mandy, then back to him. With a tinge of disdain coloring her voice, she said, "Ones who appreciate the finer things, expensive things, you know?"

"She does and I do, in my opinion." He squared his shoulders and laced his fingers with Mandy's to keep them from trembling. "How much?"

Frowning, the clerk asked, "Don't ya already have ..."

"I already told you what I need." Chaz forced himself to remain calm as he added, "Something separate. I'd like the bellman to have my luggage moved from that room to the one you're going to put me in.

Unless of course you can't help me. Perhaps your co-worker is more knowledgeable." He turned toward a red-haired woman who stood near the landline watching the incident unfold.

Her eyes widened as Chaz leaned in to read her nametag. At the same time, he gave Mandy's hand an encouraging squeeze. "Lynae? Such a lovely name. Lynae, I need a suite. The very best one you have. Your coworker seems ill-equipped. Perhaps you ... will you help me?"

Sondra's eyebrows shot up as she moved closer to Lynae. "What makes you so sure we 'ave somet'ing?" Greed sparkled in her eyes and he noticed she slipped into Patois.

"Because we wouldn't still be having this conversation if you didn't," he said, reining in his impatience. He nodded once in the direction of her coworker. "Yes, Lynae. I think you can give me what I want. One with a view, three bedrooms, connecting living area and amenities. Full service all the way. This woman was not treated right on her first day here. I'm trying to make up for that."

Sondra tried to speak, but Lynae handed her a ledger and nudged her away from the counter with her hip. "How do you know we have such a thing?"

"How much?" Chaz insisted.

She rattled off a hefty sum, and he pulled out a credit card along with some cash. "Create a different invoice from the rest of the retreat, please."

"Ah, you move fast."

She typed a few more commands into the computer, then looked up at him, but it was Sondra who was the one to quip, "Must be a really special occasion."

"It's not what you think," Mandy said, her face flushed with color. Only then did he realize how this must look to an outsider.

"Honey, it never is," Lynae countered, sliding the card and key to

Chaz. "By this time next year, you two will be in a permanent relationship. Mark my words. We'll have your things moved straight away. Hers too, if you like. She's in a standard room right below your new suite."

"Come," he said to Mandy, whose shocked expression said everything as she handed over her key card as well. "Let's start your first session."

She stared at him with wide eyes. "But did you hear ..."

Chaz pulled her closer, placing the back of her hand against his heart.

"Mandy, come with me, please. It doesn't matter what they think, it matters what you know."

Yes, he heard what Lynae had said but her words were simply the musings of a meddlesome woman and Sondra's quips were those of a nosy woman who had no clue about him or Mandy.

Mandy tore her gaze from the woman, one whose sly smile shared with her fellow desk worker didn't go unnoticed. She followed Chaz without another word but glanced over her shoulder in time to see Lynae bypass Sondra's outstretched hand and pocket the hefty tip he'd given her.

* * *

The next morning after pushing thoughts of Chaz and their time together to the background, the resort arranged private transport for Mandy back to the airport. This time, those same officers escorted her through customs and straight to the plane. They even had the nerve to tell her, "Come back again real soon."

"Not if I can help it," she said under her breath.

Even though she was scheduled for two connecting flights instead of the one non-stop, which was originally booked, she was happy to put Jamaica in her rearview mirror and touch down in the States.

* * *

When her flight landed in Mississippi, she gathered her things and prepared to scramble to baggage claim with the rest of the passengers headed wherever, then make her connection to Chicago. A sinking feeling settled in the pit of her belly as she realized that no one was being allowed to leave the plane.

Soon, two officers boarded and swept the aisle, scanning the faces of the people who were still seated. The overhead announcement confirmed her worst fears.

"Amanda McCoy, please stand. The officers need to speak with you."

This time, she was escorted past all the curious passengers, through the terminal, and directed towards a brightly-lit room with comfortable chairs and one long table.

Security officers, however, had the same dour faces in America as they did in Jamaica. Also, before they made it the last few yards to the open door, they were already singing the same song that had been playing on the security grapevine for the past twenty-four hours. "Why did they detain you in Jamaica?"

Chapter 4

Chaz had already placed a call to his lawyer to extract him from any further business dealings with Susan, and to let the judge know that the divorce was definitely not going to be rescinded as the grey-haired man had hoped. The papers were already signed by Chaz and Susan, but the judge truly believed that one last attempt at reconciliation would be all it took for their marriage to miraculously recover.

Susan kept glancing over her shoulder at him as she walked alongside her assistant, Morgan LaRue, and the rest of her unnecessary entourage. He was still angry that Susan had made an off-hand comment to an officer in the Jamaican airport alluding to the fact that Mandy was a drug mule and had a bomb. Those words were enough to cause them to also be detained for questioning because they somehow had knowledge of Mandy's alleged illegal activities or ill intent. No matter how much Susan tried to walk it back, security didn't believe her.

Then another issue presented itself because security held them even longer when they were notified that Susan had left without fully paying the resort. When confronted by Chaz, she said, "I wasn't giving those backwards ass people all that additional money."

"You ran up all those charges for meals, parties, and upgraded accommodations, trying to make up for your outward display of ignorance." Chaz ended up footing the bill and it still meant they had to stay an additional night because they missed their flight. Not at the resort, though. They wouldn't allow Susan or her people to set foot on the grounds. Although, thanks to Lynae, Chaz was welcome to come whenever he wanted. And he took her up on the offer. Susan was unraveling faster than a ball of yarn.

Now, a day later than planned, they were finally stateside, winding their way through the terminal when a familiar form caught his eye.

Mandy was being walked through the lengthy corridors by two officers. She did not look pleased. *What the hell is going on?* He instantly separated from the pack, picking up the pace as he stalked toward the woman who had not been far from his thoughts since they parted ways the last day of the retreat.

"Where are you going," Susan yelled after him.

He didn't bother to slow his stride. Somehow, he had a feeling that what was happening to Mandy was a direct result of those careless words Susan tossed to the authorities in Jamaica, about a woman smuggling contraband into the country and carrying a bomb of some sort. She had deliberately set out to hurt the woman who had done nothing to her except expose her for a fraud.

"What's going on here?" he asked as a third officer joined the group.

Mandy glanced over her shoulder and replied, "I don't know. I told them everything I know but they keep questioning me."

He was right, Susan's handiwork all over again.

"Keep moving," one of the officers said, trying to block Chaz from getting to Mandy.

She complied, but said, "First, in Jamaica they pulled me off the plane and forced me to stay an extra day. Then when I made it here, we barely touched down at the gate before they came on the plane to escort me off in front of everyone. Like I'm a criminal. I'm so tired of this."

One of the officers shared a glance with the one standing next to him who nodded. Finally, one of them said, "They found a body in the hotel room right below your suite." He glanced at his cell. "And someone mentioned that you might have drugs or explosives. That's a credible threat. When we assume that something isn't true, is when chaos ensues."

"I'm getting her a lawyer," Chaz said, rubbing his temple.

The officers froze and focused on Chaz, then looked over at Mandy. "Is this man your advocate? Ma'am, you can certainly *ask* for an attorney, but to be honest you don't have any rights here. We are a different branch of law enforcement. And there is the fact that she voluntarily submitted to a blood test and a search in Jamaica. Is it your intention now to request a lawyer and make this harder on you?"

Mandy blanched under the man's harsh gaze.

"Voluntarily?" Chaz said, tilting his head at the man. "Why are on earth would she do that?"

Mandy planted her feet and frustrated their efforts to move her forward.

"Then can you at least say why the authorities keep detaining her?" Chaz demanded, his skin flushing with heat. "Especially when the Jamaican authorities cleared her to fly. Let her go home."

"We can't let her do that just yet," the brunette tossed her response over one shoulder.

"Why?" Chaz demanded, shifting so he was a few feet away.

"I'm not at liberty to divulge that information to you," the brunette growled and tightened her grip on Mandy's arm.

"Hey," Mandy said, trying to wiggle free. "That hurts."

"Then can we get someone who can divulge that information to us," Chaz shot back, unlocking the woman's fingers from Mandy's arm. "She's not speaking to another person without counsel. Do you understand me?"

Mandy nodded, obviously relieved that someone was finally on her side.

"Mind your business," the dark-haired male officer snapped.

"She *is* my business." Chaz pulled Mandy out of their clutches. "She came to Jamaica for our retreat. Now you're not telling her why you keep doing the things you do. Other than there's a body and her name isn't attached to it. This is not fair. We want real answers and you won't give them."

"They stripped me," she choked out. "Took blood and ... please just tell me why you keep detaining me? I told you everything I know about what happened that night."

"Wait a minute," he said, after taking in her words. His head snapped to the officers. "You strip-searched her, humiliated her, and *still* no answers?"

"That wasn't us," the blonde protested and held her hands up in surrender as she shared a speaking glance with the others.

"It wasn't them," Mandy admitted. "It was the ones on the island, but it started this way and escalated to something else."

Chaz moved until he stood in front of Mandy and blocked the officers from her. "Strip search? That has to be a violation of some kind. Is that what we're doing now? Treating people like criminals without any proof whatsoever?" He sighed, exhaling a little of his frustration before saying, "Can I speak to the three of you privately for a moment?"

They hesitated a minute, then followed him off to the side, out of Mandy's hearing range.

"My wife was jealous and angry and has a poor sense of humor.

She made some tacky uncalled-for comments about explosive devices in reference to Ms. McCoy at the airport," he said to them. "Does this have anything to do with—"

"We tend to take comments about explosive devices very seriously," he said in a grave tone. "As a precaution, we check the person making the claim and the accused, here and abroad. Ms. McCoy also needs to speak with us concerning that other matter. So if you would excuse us—"

"Mandy's been on this carousel for long enough," Chaz snapped. "Contact the people in Jamaica. I promise that you'll find that Mandy isn't guilty of anything you're thinking of. If she didn't have explosives there, she didn't suddenly pick some up at the duty-free store along the way."

The three officers moved a few feet away to hold a private conversation. After a time, the shortest of the crew came back and said, "All right. We can allow her to remain here while we sort things out, but she will have to leave her passport and identification with us."

"Why?" Chaz demanded, taking Mandy's hand in his.

"As I said, we take every precaution to ensure the safety of our guests. Explosive devices are not a laughing matter. Ms. McCoy has to remain in the city. Those are the terms. In the interim, Ms. McCoy has graciously offered to assist us with another matter."

"What other matter?" His head swiveled toward Mandy, then back to the officer. "You're saying that she has to stay here, with *no* identification, which means she's not able to secure a place to stay?"

"Or she can continue the questioning right now and go home," the male officer explained.

"When?" Chaz demanded.

"Eventually."

"Please, Chaz. I'm just tired," Mandy whispered, her soft brown eyes glossy with unshed tears. "Let me keep going so they can be done. I don't want any more trouble."

Chaz pulled her close and whispered. "Mandy, have you done anything different here than in Jamaica?"

She shook her head. But her mind raced as she tried to digest everything. "Went for the workshop. Stayed to myself. They just keep asking the same things over and over, expecting a different answer. And I don't have one. Someone was hurt at the hotel and they said blood was on my doorknob and on the doorframe." She shook her head. "They thought the blood upstairs was also mine but it's not and none of this is making sense, but I have to go with them."

"Blood? Wait a minute, what? You need some rest, honey," he said, cupping her face in his hands. He was at a loss to explain why this woman he didn't know affected him so much, but there it was. "And let them figure things out all the way around, all right?"

Mandy sighed her frustration, then looked up at him and said, "All right."

"She'll return in the morning."

Under the intense gazes of the security personnel, Chaz led her in the opposite direction. "The nearest place is attached to the airport. I'll reserve your room, it's the least I can do."

"I have enough cash to take care of things," she said, squaring her shoulders. "I'm fine."

"I insist. You wouldn't be in this position if Susan hadn't made that crack about a bomb. You were already past security and waiting to board when she said something to the airline personnel out of spite."

Mandy's eyes widened with shock. "Is that why they keep—no wait, you don't understand. They're just telling me, because you insisted, that there was a body found at the hotel. I thought I heard a gunshot and I reported it to the front desk …" She inhaled and let it out slowly. "I was excluded from the investigation because the bloodwork that came back wasn't mine…" She held up her hand to ward off any further protest from him. "Never mind. I can handle this … you go… Don't you have other workshops …"

He placed a hand over hers to keep her calm. "Nothing is more important than you. I'll contact a lawyer friend in Chicago. He'll connect me with someone here."

"Thank you," she said in a much lower tone. "You've been so kind. You don't have to do this."

"I want to." He studied her tired eyes and the lines of exhaustion etched around them. "You really need some rest."

"Facts. I've never been so weary in my life," she said, exhaling. "This is like a never-ending nightmare."

He forced a smile he didn't feel. "We'll get to the bottom of it, no worries. Let's grab a meal."

"Room service, please. I just need to lay down," she said, rubbing her temples.

Chaz placed a hand on the small of her back. "Whatever you need."

"Thank you."

He checked her into an upscale hotel attached to the airport and settled her on the sofa, all while ignoring calls from Susan, Morgan, and the rest of her people. Despite Mandy's protests, he ran her a bath and put in a little of the jasmine scented soap once the water level reached above the jets. He pressed the on button and soon a white froth of bubbles filled the tub to the brim. Candles were situated nearby and he lit them so that an ethereal glow permeated the bath. This would definitely put her in a relaxed state of mind.

Chaz mulled over the interesting turn of events. He didn't feel inconvenienced in any way by helping Mandy, especially since he figured Susan had a hand in this new round of trouble.

And what was that about blood on her door? Chaz squinted as he tried to remember whether he heard anything out of the ordinary, but nothing came to mind.

After shutting off the water in the tub and finding it much too hot for the skin, he peeked in at Mandy and her head was laid back against the cushions. He made a quick trek to the nearby hotel where he was originally supposed to stay, aiming to pick up the remainder of his belongings.

From where he stood in the lobby, he could see Susan pacing back and forth in the bar with her cell clutched in her hand. She pressed something on the screen and seconds later his cell vibrated again.

One nasty public display was enough to last a lifetime. Judging from the way she swayed on her feet as she reached for and barely missed a wine flute, that public display was all she wanted. Lights, cell phone, camera and she would be on, crying crocodile tears and adding fuel to the proverbial fire.

No, he wouldn't give her the satisfaction of starring in her drama.

Chaz side-stepped the front desk, headed straight for VIP Concierge and asked, "Could you quietly bring the front desk manager over please."

"Sure thing. I'm here to help."

She slid by him, walked the distance past the building line of people waiting for check in, then disappeared into an area behind the busy front office people. When she returned with a tall, leggy blonde, he smiled, handed over his identification and said, "I need a huge favor."

Moments after she listened to his request and the reason that things needed to be kept on the "sneak tip" she went to the front desk and whispered something to a woman typing into at a console. A few minutes later, the front desk manager slid him the key to the suite that had been reserved for him and directed a bellman upstairs to help with retrieving his luggage.

On such a quick trip in and out, he couldn't locate one important item—that journal that was still missing in action, but as the moments ticked by, he thought better of lingering to put his hands on that small toiletry bag where it might be.

"Let's make moves," he said to his newfound bellman friend. They were stepping into another elevator when he could swear Susan's angry voice was making its distance up the hallway. The decision to leave the rest of his things behind had been a great instinct.

The bellman smirked and held out his fist for a pound. Chaz chuckled and obliged by tapping his fist on the darker man's.

Chaz hurried back to the hotel near the airport and ordered the toiletry items he needed at the front desk before heading up to the suite he shared with Mandy.

Susan had destroyed any hope whatsoever of reconciling, or that such a "high profile" marriage could find its way to becoming whole as the judge wanted. No way could he remain with her after the way she showed her entire ass.

Elitist. Racist. Prejudiced. How could he have missed those parts of her? He'd been taken by the biggest con of the century and she was still trying to keep her hooks in him.

Chapter 5

Chaz refreshed the water in the tub, scooped Mandy's sleeping form from the sofa and at first, he simply stood there holding her. She fit against the core of him as if the Creator fashioned her especially for him. Chaz breathed in the soft earthy scent of her and smiled as he carried her into the bathroom. She opened her eyes and locked in on his. Mandy instinctively threw her arms around his neck as her gaze darted about.

"What are you doing?"

"Hush, Mandy, I have no intention of dropping you."

"Wait Chaz… I don't under—" She struggled in his arms.

Chaz stood still and cradled her to his chest.

"Shhhh, Mandy. I'm just making sure you wash away all of this negativity, so you'll have a peaceful night's sleep."

She gave him a half smile. "I can get with that."

He gently perched her on the edge of the tub and asked, "Are you going to be all right?"

"I think so," she whispered. "It sure looks good in here. Are you trying to make me fall in love with you?"

"Hadn't thought of anything like that, but now that you mention it …"

She gave a low throaty chuckle that warmed his heart.

"I'll leave you to it."

"And here it is, I thought this was a full-service hotel."

Chaz paused on his way to the door. "Mandy, my kind of full service would mean a tongue bath so long and so thorough that neither one of us would see the light of day for the next week," he said. "Behave yourself."

"And now you're cursing at me."

"What?"

"You said behave."

Chaz lowered his gaze to her lips, crossed the distance between them before leaning in to press his lips to hers. She welcomed him in for a luscious taste of the moistness within and it took everything within him to pull away.

"No, beloved, you're travel weary and in no condition to make a rational decision when it comes to this. When we cross that threshold into something more … something *beautiful*, I want you fully awake and aware of every decision we make. I want to taste every line and curve of you. I want to know the feel of your open mouth on my skin worshiping me the way I long to worship you. Anything else is beneath you."

She inhaled sharply and whispered a breathy, "You have such a way with words."

"And that ain't all," he said with a wink, causing her to chuckle.

Several minutes later, room service wheeled in trays of chef's salads, chicken marsala, pilaf, margherita pizza, chocolate-covered strawberries, and vanilla shortcake for dessert. Chaz stood in the alcove where they placed the food holding the phone to one ear, the other listening out for the sounds of water splashes in the bathroom to signal that Mandy hadn't fallen asleep.

"Make that call to the judge and let him know that things are done on my end," he said to Sonya Holland, his divorce lawyer who finally returned his call. "We've never squabbled over money. Everything was already split down the middle. She stalled on certain properties and to end this without drawing it out, I let her have them. No excuses. I want to be totally free."

Sonya was silent so long, Chaz thought she'd disconnected the call until she said, "Are you absolutely, positively sure?"

"The judge only held out, believing there was one last chance for us. There. Is. None."

"So that means I have to place a call to Joshua…"

"And cancel anything else we had in the works with Susan." He grabbed a strawberry off the tray and popped it in his mouth, knowing that Joshua Naples, his corporate attorney, was not going to be elated at the news. "Even those here in the South."

"You know the women actually come to see you."

"But they pay to see *her*," Chaz countered, undeterred in his decision. "That's how she wanted it. I was only there for support. If she can't carry the business under her own steam, then that's going to be something she'll need to compensate for. I'm not doing it any longer. I've served my time in a loveless marriage."

"Let me come to you," Sonya pleaded. "Let's talk about things. This is going to hurt your business as well."

"There's *nothing* to discuss. The judge said that this time, all we had to do was call and my signature on the papers would be valid and entered into the court's system. He's holding them hostage in his chambers and the court is still open. The marriage *and* partnership are both over. If he doesn't respect that, then I'll take the copy that I have and we'll go to another judge and get this done." He placed a slice of pizza along with some of the chef's salad onto a white plate.

"How are we going to spin this for the media?" Sonya scoffed.

"However she likes," he said. "I couldn't care less what tale she sees fit to tell. Good night."

"Wait—"

Chaz disconnected the call and felt a weight lifted from his heart and mind. All the resentment and anger. Every ounce seemed to leave his body with this one last action toward freedom.

He peered into the bedroom, only to find a half-nude Mandy stretched out diagonally on the bed like a teenager. The plush throw from the bottom of the bed was slung partially over her top half, as though she had fallen asleep in the middle of covering herself. He placed the plate of food on the nightstand next to her.

Vulnerable. Beautiful.

Chaz had come across many women in his career; had been photographed with ones who were considered the most gorgeous and exotic in the world. None of them were as captivating as the sleeping beauty lying before him. He wished things were different and he could undress and join her, or wake her with an excruciatingly slow nip along the back of her thighs.

No, beloved, when I make you mine you must be awake. I want you to know and never forget me…us… this night and forever.

Chaz smoothed the blanket over her bottom and stepped back from the bed.

Her eyelids fluttered, then she looked at him with a sleep-filled gaze. "What's a hall pass?" she asked, her voice breathy and husky from sleep.

Chaz frowned, unsure why she locked onto that subject. "Mandy?"

She stared at him, waiting.

"It's where a spouse gives their partner permission to sleep with another person."

"And she gave you one?"

"Yes, but she's no longer my—"

"So, sleep with me," she whispered. "The bed is big enough for both of us. You have one side. I'll be on the other. You know where your parts are and I know where my parts are and neither the twain shall …"

She drifted off again.

Chaz didn't have the heart to correct her words. Instead, he tipped out of the room to make one last phone call before he turned in. He needed some distance to get a handle on his feelings for Mandy.

She had been his most diligent client to date. She had struggled with spiritual concepts, and the yoga poses at first, and he worked with her using a different approach. First, meditation—and it took her a long time to quiet the chatter going on in her mind. The self-consciousness about her body—in her eyes, seen as imperfect—was the biggest challenge. He formulated a series of foundational poses to increase balance and flexibility. Every successful move brought on the biggest smile, and it warmed his heart.

Susan somehow found out where he was staying and had tried to create chaos during the sessions by showing up to interrupt them. That came to a screeching halt when he warned that if she did it again, he wouldn't show for any of the evening sessions that were strictly slated for professionals, either.

Speaking of Susan's assistant, Morgan deserved a courtesy call because the moment he didn't show for the next workshop in Natchez, the shit was going to hit the fan and it wouldn't be evenly distributed.

The phone rang for half a second before Morgan came on the line. "Chaz, what in hell?!"

"It's time. Waaaaay past time," he said, peering into the bedroom to check on Mandy. "I found out some things about Susan that were unforgivable."

Morgan inhaled sharply. "She told you about the babies?"

"She could've been honest about that a long time ago."

"I told her she should tell you," she countered. "But she insisted that you shouldn't know. It was women's business."

Somehow, he had the feeling they were talking about two separate things. "Babies are everyone's business," he hedged, waiting for her to give more insight.

"And y'all would've had some cute ones if she hadn't ended those pregnancies."

"True, but..." the last three words hit home. "Wait a minute, did you say pregnancies as in plural? Multiple?"

"Yes, I thought you said you found out about the abortions." Morgan's voice dropped by a notch. "All three of them."

This time it was Chaz who inhaled, and let it out slowly, almost with a death grip on the cell. But the chill spreading to his bones wouldn't subside.

"Chaz?"

"Yes, I'm here." His words were faint and he sat to prevent himself from falling.

"You didn't know?" she gasped. "Oh, my Lord, she's going to kill me."

Chaz didn't have any reason to, but allaying her fears might eventually work in his favor. "I won't tell where I got the information."

"Thank you."

"But I'm also going to need you to lay low on the smear tactics when you take this public."

"You know she'll go for the jugular," Morgan warned. "Between me and you, if you let her out of the gate first, then she's going to shape the narrative."

Chaz glanced into the other room again. "I don't care about any of that."

"You should," Morgan shot back. "It's going to cost you money if she makes you look like the bad guy."

He sucked in a breath. "How many abortions?"

"I mentioned three. Those are just the ones she told me about. One miscarriage that first year. That one's a little suspect if you ask me."

Four possible children during their marriage; knowing what he wanted. "Yet, I'm the bad guy."

"Chaz, get your publicist on her job and fashion the narrative or that's how the world—and people who've been following you—are going to see it. That you're a man just like all the others and you're no different for all your spiritual talk."

"We both know that's not the case."

"Yes, but they don't."

* * *

Mandy turned over, situated the pillow into a better position, reflecting on that first day with Chaz which became a turning point in her life . . .

"Chaz, really," Mandy protested, following him into the suite. *"This is a bit much."*

"You deserve better," he said, and he guided her to an outdoor patio. The warm tropical breeze was heavy with the scent of jasmine orchids and ylang ylang. *"Your stay started off not so great. Let's see if I can make things right."*

The view was magnificent. All bright blue skies and sand. The suite's amenities were a far cry from the meager ones in her standard room below. Something she could never afford with her limited finances. She didn't even know this type of opulence existed. And he wanted her to stay here with him? Just the two of them? With that hellion of a ... whoever she was ... gunning for her? Not likely.

When they stepped back inside the air-conditioned space, Chaz settled on the center of the living room floor. With one hand, he beckoned her to join him.

"On second thought," Mandy said. "This whole private session thing might not work for me."

"Oh?" he said with a smile. "You have somewhere else you have to be?"

"It's just ... I—"

"Mandy, give it a try first," he said in a voice that held a tinge of a British accent. "Then if it doesn't work for you, we'll try something that does."

She gazed at the purple orchids that were a stark contrast to the turquoise and cream décor. "Five minutes."

"I'll only take four," he said with a smile. "Come."

Mandy soon sat in the lotus position, facing Chaz.

"Tell me why you came," he said, and there was a sincerity in his voice that touched her.

She shrugged and let her hands fall in her lap. "Actually, I thought yoga was a white-folks thing."

"Everyone does yoga."

Shaking her head, Mandy claimed, "Never laid eyes on a yoga instructor that looked anything like me."

Chaz chuckled. "And where, exactly, did you look?"

"That's beside the point," she said, averting her gaze to the plush carpet.

"Mandy, look at me," he whispered.

She took a moment to comply, but when she did, he continued, "Part of what you're feeling about this whole experience stems from what you feel about yourself. So let's deal with that issue."

"All right."

"What is the biggest challenge you have when it comes to your body?"

She lowered her gaze to the hand he placed on her arm. "I've struggled with weight issues all my life. I've been fighting, and it's been winning." She closed her eyes a moment, filtering through to the truth of the matter. Then she opened her eyes and focused on him. "I think it might be a shield and a security blanket. I thought it would keep the men in my family from ..." She looked away and tears glazed her eyes. "I mention it first to save others the trouble. 'Elephant in the room has nothing on me.' It's a joke I used to say to get a laugh. It was my buy-in, either that or an apology for the inconvenience of my existence. It's been that way so long, that almost every experience in my adult life is a mirror image of how I felt about myself growing up."

He winced as a slash of something that might have been pain pierced his heart on hearing her words; the savage beauty of her vulnerability laid bare. At that moment, he wanted to do everything in his power to protect her from anything, or anyone else, who could harm her.

"I heard Wayne Dyer speak once when he was diagnosed," Mandy said, finally looking him in the eyes again. "In a powerful motivational talk, he said he made a decision that he and the cancer would co-exist. That said a lot. I made the decision that me and the fat would become friends. A few days later, I went to the doctor and she looked at my chart and said, 'you've dropped ten pounds, what are you doing?' I said, 'the hell if I know, I'm as shocked as you are'."

Chaz chuckled along with her, then took her hands in his. "Mandy, I think you need to look at things from a different perspective. Our bodies are simply what we choose to take this spiritual journey through life. Some of us choose the sports car models, some—"

"The SUV model," *Mandy supplied.*

"*I was going to say luxury model, but even SUVs come in luxury form as well,*" *he said, with an encouraging smile.* "*You're so busy looking at the outside, you don't understand the real work is on the inside. Yoga, meditation, and mantra starts work from the inside out. Over the next few days, we'll focus on all three—quieting your mind with meditation, helping you become more flexible with basic yoga poses, and calming the things that you're worried about to effect a change, with mantra.*" *Her fingers curled around his and he took that as an encouraging sign as he said,* "*There's a song beneath your skin, a love story that's a lifetime in the making. And that story begins with loving yourself, then letting others love you.*" *He gave those delicate manicured fingers a gentle squeeze.* "*Are you open to that? Are you open to trying?*"

Mandy remained silent for so long, he didn't think she would answer. Then ...

"*Yes, Chaz,*" *she whispered.* "*I think I am.*"

Chapter 6

"Where the hell is he? He never leaves his shaving kit. I mean, how did he manage to get the rest of his things out of here so quickly? I always unpack and he never leaves his kit behind, ever," Susan screeched, glaring at the hand-crafted furniture holding the offensive piece of Chaz's belongings.

Morgan ran one thumb over her phone screen. "He's not answering his phone or responding to texts."

Obviously. Susan paced a fevered yard in front of the widescreen television. "When was the last time you heard anything?"

Her assistant, best friend, and confidant, looked down her narrow nose and said, "When he broke rank in order to help that woman. This is not good. Your patrons are going to hit the roof."

Susan's anger shot to an all-time high, when she realized Morgan was right. "Well, they don't pay to see him," she snapped, knowing that the opposite was true. "They'll get over it."

Morgan was smart enough to keep her mouth shut.

"I can't have another mishap after what happened in Jamaica,"

Susan said, still perturbed at what transpired. How had things gone so horribly wrong? She wasn't racist. She had a lot of Black friends. Well, a handful. Okay, it had been taken down to two when she'd said something that she couldn't walk back. One of them had warned her that if she ever got busted saying some racist crap, not to count her in that "I've got Black friends" number. But still.

"Nearly half the class walked out," she mused, picturing that last near-empty room. "The rest were not as responsive because of what he did."

"Get it right," Morgan snapped, looking up from her phone screen. "You mean, what you did?"

"No, what *he* did," Susan snarled. "He should've let her walk out."

"You need to own up to your shit," Morgan said, her tone uncompromising. She flipped her hair over one shoulder. "You screwed up. Showed some things that made everyone uncomfortable. Hell, I would've walked too." Morgan snatched up her electronic tablet. "*You people*."

"Oh, I didn't mean it that way," Susan said, waving her off.

Morgan's nostrils flared. She was more pissed off than Susan realized.

"You people. Then what did you mean?" Morgan asked. "Given the social climate, those were the wrong words to toss out there. And Chaz was right, that was just enough for people to see your true mindset. Culturally insensitive. Totally tone deaf. No wonder he had to do damage control."

Susan wondered what those private sessions with Chaz had entailed. Instead of being by her side on day two, three, and four, he was hidden away with that unwanted guest. And her class size kept dwindling. Every. Single. Day. Susan never realized how important Chaz was to her business. The fear that they would fold altogether was looming as a stark reality. She had banked her entire career on their being together, because Chaz, unlike her previous husband, was loyal. Well, past tense. Evidently that loyalty was gone. He even went so far as to have the resort provide him with a separate suite altogether on that first afternoon. Maybe Morgan was right. She should have issued an apology before Chaz left with that woman.

One of the participants came up to Susan and said, "My father is Black. I may look White, and so do some of the others. But trust me, we have Black people in our family."

Who knew?

Susan had always been more concerned with women who gravitated to Chaz. She did her part to let the world know he belonged to her. Any time he posted on Social Media, Susan was right there, posting her comments to let everyone know he was her "hunny bunny", "soul mate", "sweet cheeks", and her "forever love". No mistaking who he belonged to.

Morgan mentioned that she should lay off so much syrupy talk because it came off as insincere and mostly insecure. Especially since, even before their break, he didn't necessarily pour on the love quite the way she did. He was supportive, but reserved.

"The woman is a non-issue," Susan said, snapping back to the present.

"Keep thinking that," Morgan warned with a smirk. "Your business and your marriage will never recover."

Susan walked to the window and gazed out on the beautiful Mississippi skies. "Oh, they'll forget all about that in a few weeks."

"Really?"

She glanced over her shoulder in time to see Morgan pull up an image on an electronic tablet. "Registration for the retreat here in Jackson is down fifty percent. Requests for refunds—within the deadline—are up three times that amount. We're going to have to cancel the California class, as well as the Atlanta and New York ones. England and Dubai will be next."

"California?" Susan croaked as her heart did a strange tango against her chest wall.

"Yes, your home base," she said, her expression hard and unforgiving. "That should be of particular concern. Racism is not respected anywhere, Susan. You belittled that woman after she pointed out your blatant lie. Why you couldn't have been humble and just apologize is beyond me."

Morgan shook her head, the blonde curls accentuated every move. Then she tossed the tablet onto the sofa and crossed her legs. "But hey, what do I know. You're the star, right? No matter how dim it is."

Chapter 7

Chaz left the living room, switched off his phone, and stood at the bedside looking down at Mandy. "Permission to hold you?" he whispered.

Mandy's eyes flew open and locked in on his. In a husky voice, she said, "Permission granted."

He slid off his shirt and shoes, then lay next to her. Chaz inhaled the soapy scent coming off her skin and prepared to sleep. Then she stretched languidly until she was curved into him. The luscious feel of those curves pressed against him sent a range of sensations pulsing through his body.

"Good night," she whispered. "Sweet dreams."

Chaz smiled and released a contented sigh. "I'm having one."

She was asleep within seconds.

The days he had spent teaching her the basics, then more advanced ways of stretching, flexibility, and meditation, were the most pleasurable he had experienced in a while. Seeing her progress and the elation on her face when she succeeded was well worth it. The third day in, as she became more secure, he moved their sessions to the beach. Being in such close proximity was doing a number on him. The attraction became stronger each passing hour. But being in the open might not have been the best choice as some of Susan's guests zeroed in on them and sought him out . . .

"*Do you mind if I join you?*" a slender woman asked, running a hand through her raven tresses.

Chaz saw the moment Mandy tensed and he said, "Actually, we do."

"*This is not fair.*" Kim pouted and her British accent thickened, signaling her disappointment. "*We came to this because the two of you present together.*"

"*Now we're settling for half of that,*" another woman complained, raising her voice over the wind coming off the Caribbean Sea. A gaggle of people approached them, plodding through the white sand.

"*She has the message.*" Chaz spared Mandy a glance, then focused on Susan's guest. "*That should be your focus.*"

"*It's not the same,*" Emma whispered, her bright blue eyes pleading her case more than her words.

Chaz waved one hand to encompass the sand. "*None of what she offers is happening out here.*"

Kim folded her arms. "*I'm fine with that.*"

"*I'm not,*" Chaz said, meeting her gaze.

Kim glared at Mandy and so did others. "*What makes her so special?*"

"*Is something going on here?*" one of the men said, flickering a gaze between Mandy and Chaz.

"*Nothing out of the ordinary,*" Chaz answered in a firm voice. "*Have a nice day,*"

"He said no," the man told the others who trekked across the sand behind him.

Groans went up among them. Then the insurrection started.

"I think I'm going to take the first flight back to Peru. The energy has been off since day one."

"She's not going to refund our money."

"I don't care about that, but it's the last dollars she'll get from me."

Chaz realized that Susan's people would have difficulty adjusting to his absence. He had been insisting for a while that they needed to split their business interests to ensure that their brands stayed individually intact. That was more for Susan's benefit since they had different ideals when it came to healing. His following had developed because of his motivational speaking, books, and life coaching sessions with celebrities. Hers took a major upswing when he became involved.

"Chaz, you spend so much time putting your energy into healing others," Mandy said, snatching his thoughts back to their present moment. "When do you give to yourself? You're always talking about what I deserve and to release the past so I can be happy. Don't you deserve to be happy, too?" She reached out and cupped his face in her hands. "You're more than just the face of that company or a picture in a magazine. You're so much more than that. If you're challenging me to move forward in life, then I'm going to lay that on you as well. I need you to practice what you preach."

As the group trudged back to the resort, defeat registering with every step, he realized that Mandy was right. He had felt some remorse over making such an abrupt departure from this event.

But only a little.

***

Sunlight streamed into the suite, bathing her in warmth. Mandy opened her eyes. Two things hit her at once. *Hall pass. Sleep with me.*

She scrambled out of Chaz's arms and from the bed. When she stood next to it, she looked down at the unfamiliar clothes on her body. Then it hit her—*his clothes* that she commandeered after her bath.

He shifted and in the next moment, those piercing dark-brown eyes focused on her. "What's wrong?"

Chaz was on his feet in a second, scanning the room for signs of danger.

"Hall pass," she whispered, combing one hand through her hair. "It meant making love, right?"

The smile that lifted his lips was blinding in its intensity. He settled onto the bed, then leaned back onto the pillows. "Yes, it does, But—"

"I didn't mean," she inhaled, placing a hand on her heart. "I never ... I—"

"Mandy, I know, honey," he said in the calmest tone he could manage. "Your explanation showed you were not aware of the true meaning. At least, not then."

She sighed her relief. "I apologize. I didn't mean to lead you on."

"I didn't think that for a moment. You were tired."

"So, we didn't ..." she hedged, one eyebrow raised.

"Mandy, if we had made love last night," he replied, all of the humor leaving his voice. "Trust me, you would know. I wouldn't take advantage of a woman who is not in the mind to consent. I simply asked permission to hold you—nothing more advanced than what we have done in sessions where we were that close. The adrenaline was still rushing through your body — even asleep. In—"

"I mean, it's not that I don't want you in that way, I do," she confessed, and suddenly felt embarrassed that she shared that information, especially given his relationship with Susan. "And that scares me."

Chaz left the bed and faced her. "Seriously? I wouldn't hurt you."

"I don't know that. I just want to get back to my calm, predictable life. Especially after what I've been through. Sure you want to be seen with someone like me?" She'd meant it as a joke, but the frown on his face made her sober up.

Chaz reached for her hand, stroking the finger that was missing the tell-tale sign that she belonged to someone. "Married?"

"Why do you need to know?" she asked. "Especially given your questionable marriage."

"There is no marriage," he said, his voice darkening with anger. "The divorce papers were signed a few weeks ago but entering them in the system is being held up by a judge who feels we should get past our issues and reconcile. So, answer my question."

Married? Hell no! Worst mistake of her entire life.

She remembered sitting in the compact office of the lawyer she hired eight years ago when it became clear that Kenny was just using her. The lawyer, Tom Selleck—who looked nothing like the gorgeous actor—had put a private investigator on the case.

"I've got good news and bad news."

"Give me the bad news," she said.

"Your husband has purchased several big-ticket items using your social security number."

"I'm confused," she said. "How is that even possible? Doesn't someone from the mortgage company have to verify employment and all of that? Same with the people who financed the car. Fifteen, maybe twenty years ago, I could see someone getting away with that. That's because the average Jolene didn't know much about identity theft."

"Unless you count parents that opened utilities and credit cards in their children's names because they jacked up their own. My mother did that to a few of my sisters. They couldn't finance things because they had so many negative hits on their credit. And because they weren't willing to fill out a police report and take my mother to court, what she had done would stand. Nowadays, it's hard to get something on credit for yourself, let alone using someone else's information."

"Your options are not going to be pleasant. I obtained your credit report so you can check and see if he did anything else," Mr. Selleck explained. "Today, we'll make a call, then put in documentation to place a freeze on all three credit reports. Nothing else will be approved on any level without extended measures. I'll draft a letter to your creditors as you repair the damage he's done. We'll also contact the police and file a criminal complaint."

She sank down into the chair. "Seriously?"

"Yes ma'am," Mr. Selleck replied. "That's going to be something that's required. Don't expect much help from them because this takes a back seat to other crimes, and this one is a lot more common. We have to give the police report to each of the creditors as part of the claim about what Kenny did. That'll let you off the hook for any action he took without your knowledge and consent. And I'll prepare a lawsuit to put the finance company on the hook, we'll also file a Federal Trade Commission complaint. Your creditors will want that. Crimes like these reach the federal level. You may need this as evidence that it wasn't you who did these things."

"I don't see why he did this," she said, scanning the report. "He's supposed to have his own business."

Mr. Selleck's head jerked up and his green eyes settled on hers. "Let's check Illinois corporate filings to see if he used your identity for anything else. While obtaining personal credit is hard, setting up a company using someone else's identity is a lot easier. Your husband may have been using your good name to rip folks off."

"I can't believe this," she said, slumping further in the seat. "He's my husband, we're supposed to be a team. It's not supposed to be like this."

This was the day the last bit of shine wore off of the ideal of marriage for Mandy. The steps she would have to take to protect herself and her good name meant her husband would be brought up on Federal charges. The issue strengthened her resolve to fully end things. Their pastor intervened, insisting that they come in for counseling.

After several weeks, Mandy reversed the actions she had started to prosecute, but doing so also dragged her name and credit through the mud before the smoke finally cleared.

Marriage? Hell no, in all capital letters.

Chaz's gentle hold on her shoulder woke Mandy from the trance she'd fallen into.

"Married once," she said, answering Chaz's question. "Divorced him long ago."

"You haven't had someone in your life since then?"

"No. No intimate relationships," she confessed. "Not since the last men tried to—" Her chest heaved as she made the effort to wrap her lips around a word she preferred not to say.

Chaz enfolded her hand in his warm grip. "What happened?"

She leveled a hard gaze on him and said, "I killed them."

Chapter 8

Chaz continued to ignore the flood of calls and texts from Susan. Instead, he waited for Mandy to shower and dress before she joined him in the living room. He guided her through a series of yoga poses to relax her. That confession when she first woke up seemed to take the wind out of her. He didn't press any further. She would tell him more about her marriage and that horrific experience in time ... *I killed them.* He couldn't imagine what had transpired to cause something so drastic.

Last night, he had washed her clothes and hung them over the shower bar; then made a note that they would go shopping first thing in the morning. She slid into another one of his shirts, which was stretched sensuously across her full breasts to the point he ached simply from the sight of her nipples jutting toward the material. Her body was lush and sexy. Something he could definitely sink into and stay forever.

"Forgive me for not asking you before I stepped in and took over, I ..."

She shook her head, took his hands in hers. "I like that you've actively shown that you have my best interests at heart. Even drawing me a bath, candles, and all that. It was beautiful. Amazing even." Then her gaze narrowed on him. "But if you had taken it a step further and actually picked up the sponge and—"

"No, ma'am," he said with a chuckle, "I wasn't going that far, unless …"

"Well, to be honest, I think I would have liked that." She gave him a warm smile. "Something that would have been a first time for me. And why not? You've taken care of everything else. What's a little intimacy between ... friends."

He leaned in to press a kiss to her lips, and a little worry settled in his heart. He had gone about this all wrong. "And also being honest, I should apologize to you. I should never have let my attraction to you cloud my professional judgement. You're a client and that is not how things are done, but there's something … I can't even describe it, but—"

"So now I'm a client?" she folded her arms across her ample breasts.

"Correction. You *were* a client. Now you're so much more."

"What's the matter," she asked, pausing to adjust his shirt over her midriff.

His gaze swept across her curves and he shifted next to her on the sofa. "That looks better on you than it ever did on me."

"It is a little snug, though."

"Yes," he whispered, now trying to keep his gaze on her face and his erection under control. Her nipples hardened and it took everything within him not to answer their call to tease them, touch them, taste them. This woman was sending him into a frenzy of need. A need that had gone unmet for far too long.

"Why are you looking at me like that?" she asked. "Like you want to …"

"Because I do."

She inched backward, staring at him in shock, then put her focus on her hands. "No, that can't be possible."

"Why?" he answered, causing her to look up at him. Mandy quickly averted her gaze, this time focusing on the swirl patterns in the carpet.

"Face me," he commanded.

She complied, but the heat between them demanded every ounce of self-control.

"Why do you have such a hard time with the fact that a man could be attracted to you? Could desire you? Tell me."

Chaz lifted her chin with his finger so their gazes met.

"Why, Mandy?"

"Because I don't believe you," she whispered. "Because no one ... no *man* ever has."

He pressed his lips to hers, then pulled away and lifted her hand from her lap. Gently, he guided it to the hard flesh between his thighs. "Every time I'm near you, this happens. I want you in the best way. There's something that drives me, wanting to give you pleasure; to watch as you flow into that orgasm and lose yourself completely. "

* * *

Mandy fixed her eyes on Chaz. She shifted position in an effort to contain the heat and ease the throbbing between her thighs. She hadn't let a man come anywhere near her after that horrific incident on the night she was supposed to leave Mississippi for good. The night the guards were set to deliver her to the judge's home. Something she didn't realize was part of her condition for release.

She lowered her gaze to the carpet and shook her head a little. She wasn't going to let the past invade her present and ruin this wonderful moment. Chaz had taken so much time with her on the island, trying to right a wrong that wasn't his to fix. He was charming, warm, sincere—something she didn't expect from men anymore. She tended to paint them all with a brush stroke dipped from the same can of paint. Mandy yearned to believe that he was different. That these heated looks, soft touches, and all the things he'd done for her came from a pure place.

"Look at me," he commanded.

She sighed, then met his intense stare.

"Talk to me, sweetheart." Chaz took her hands and intertwined their fingers. "Tell me what's going through your mind right now."

"It's just …"

"It's just what?" he prompted.

Mandy knew she couldn't tell Chaz what happened to her, or explain that as much as she wanted him, she was frightened. Not of him, but the fear that the nightmares would overpower their moment—as they had destroyed her life. She might not be able to handle being physically intimate with him—at least not so soon. At least, that's what reeled over and over in her mind. Yet, Mandy's body was singing another tune. She wanted him to keep the promise that his hands were making, his eyes were making, and his lips—with that one kiss—said he could deliver.

She craved him like water to cracked scorching earth. Heaven and earth collided in his molten hot gaze. The fabric holding her at bay, burned against her aching peaks. His mouth … yes, his mouth was the answer—all slick and wet. His jaws hollowing as he drew sustenance from her, teased one nipple and then the other until every nerve ending in her body sang for him … *only for him*.

"I've never had much luck with men or sex," she whispered, which was true enough. Even her ex was sorely lacking in that department. Soon as she said, "I do," seemed like all his body could say was "I can't." At least with her.

A fresh surge of hunger made her grab the side of the cushion in her fist as she tried to stand. Chaz placed a hand on her thigh, stilling her movements. He tugged gently, making her turn to face him. He shifted the soft lace of her panties, ran his thumb between the sensitive folds of her delta, making her moan and bite her lip.

"Your luck is about to change, my love." Chaz teased his tongue across her lips until her body trembled again. "Just focus on us, right here, right now. In fact, why don't you take control?"

Mandy's lips tingled from his touch. "Me?" she extracted her hands, then pointed at her chest; a move that brought a wide smile to Chaz's lips. "You want *me* to take the lead?"

"Yes," he replied, focusing those piercing, dark eyes on her so hard that she felt he was gazing into her very soul.

She held her bottom lip prisoner with her teeth, stopping the trembling. "Show me where you want me."

"I think that's a question I should be asking you. Your pleasure is my pleasure, Mandy. Tell me … show me how to please you." His brows stood at attention and Mandy saw the mischievous twinkle in his eyes. One that almost made her smile and push away all thoughts that he was playing a game that she would surely lose. "I ache for you, Mandy. So much … so very, very much. Are you aching, too? Let me make it better, beloved. Show me … tell me." He ran his thumbnail over the nub, making her jump. His eyes lit up as he leaned closer. "I'd like to kiss it … you … can I kiss it to make it better?"

She took his hand, led him to the master bedroom, and he settled on the mattress. Chaz watched as she removed her garments.

Despite the brave front she was determined to exude, she hoped he wouldn't notice that her nerves were all over the place.

Mandy stood before Chaz and his eyes darkened, breathing changed while his erection fought against his pants, clearly ready to make its grand entrance. Chaz's reaction to her was a powerful and satisfying feeling. Especially given the time that they shared in Jamaica, where he encouraged her to release any misconceptions of her worth, beauty and what she deserved. She didn't know this would be one of them.

"Damn you're amazing," he said, his voice low and husky.

"Thank you," she whispered, grateful that the words "I am?" didn't slip past her lips. During their sessions, he talked a great deal about accepting compliments—and allowing them to stand without feeling obligated to automatically return one.

His roaming gaze was like a gentle caress against her heated skin.

Feeling bold, she said, "Take off your clothes."

Chaz stood, reduced the distance between them, and held Mandy's curious stare. "As you wish, my love."

He seemed to be on automatic pilot as he held her gaze and removed each piece quickly and with precision.

Mandy was so mesmerized by the magnificence of Chaz's broad shoulders and muscled chest with its fine silky hairs she couldn't wait to touch, that she didn't realize he had also done away with his black briefs.

When she noticed his jutting erection, she gasped.

Chaz gifted her with a megawatt smile. "I take that as a—"

"Hell yes," she whispered, as her thighs grew slick with the want of him. He must have noticed because he stepped closer and ran his thumb between the sweet connection of her thighs. She watched as he gently sucked the tip.

"Mmmmm," he moaned. "My own personal honeycomb."

She needed him more than her next breath. Needed to feel beautiful … to feel something other than the pain and the hopelessness that shadowed her life. "Make love to me, Chaz."

He swept Mandy into his arms, placed her on the bed, gently laying her flat on her back.

She reached for him, and he took her fingers into his mouth, teasing the tips with his tongue. "Patience, my love."

Chaz leaned in and moistened her nipple, coiling his tongue around the erect nub. Mandy flinched, but not from fear. The fire that consumed her made it impossible to see straight. He eased her closer and laid a soft trail of kisses down to her navel, teasing her with his breath and tongue.

With both palms on the outside of her thighs, Chaz reeled Mandy in, eliciting a moan. He gripped her with a light touch, and the fire in his eyes was magical to behold.

She trembled as he lowered his head and kissed her between her thighs. Mandy closed her eyes to absorb every sensation from his warm tongue sampling her essence. She arched against him, her legs trembling.

Chaz continued his journey, tracing each letter of his name in her quivering flesh before ending each stroke with a soft, slow languid kiss. Only then did she realize Chaz wasn't just sampling her. He was savoring every inch with each pass of his tongue and lips over the sensitive pearl at the crescent of her thighs.

No, this man would never rush. If it took all night or a thousand years, this man would take his time because his pleasure was woven into the fabric of hers.

When he expertly brought her to that first orgasm, which had her shuddering against his mouth, a warm wave of wicked elixir spilled over his lips. She reached for him as he drank deeply from her primitive challis. If blood was life, her nectar was *eternal life* and the forbidden realms of ecstasy between.

As their eyes met, Chaz gently eased inside her welcoming warmth. From his slow, deliberate movements, Mandy understood he was allowing her body to stretch to accommodate him. She clung to him, staring into his eyes, mesmerized by the desire she saw in them, until they found their rhythm.

He pulled her as close as skin would allow while she whimpered into the curve of his shoulder. The heat intensified as their passion swept them away to a place where only their pleasure existed.

Much later, Chaz withdrew from her body, gathered her into his arms, and whispered, "I have to admit, I believe I'm the lucky one."

Chapter 9

I belong to you, Mandy. I feel like I always have.

A quiet, yet simple truth that settled over him as he stared up at the ceiling. There could never… would never be another. He drew the blankets around her as fantasies of growing old with her danced in his mind. As her thigh slipped between his, he felt the moisture of her skin and the moment that tears pricked her eyes.

Chaz held Mandy in his arms, relishing the feel of her next to him. Many women misunderstood who Chaz Maharaj was at his core. They tried to use him in any number of ways. Some saw him as an "exotic experience" with no intention of staying in the relationship for the long haul. Others left him the minute he made it clear he was not going to keep them in the style they desired.

He had grown up in poverty, raised by parents who had escaped arranged marriages to be together. They were disowned by both royal families because of their actions.

Struggling in Tower Hamlets in East London as his parents found their way without any financial means, set the stage where Chaz wanted to succeed at all costs. Sometimes, he remembered the days when the only entertainment was a black and white television with three channels and a slot to put fifty-pence coins in for two hours of watching time. With that background, wasting money on unnecessary material things was not his way. Experiences yes, dropping half of the money he managed to rake in on trivial things—not at all.

Always the shadow of possible failure followed his steps and actions. Even his mother did not consider his career choice a proper one. She had wanted him to work in the legal field and find a way to fight for his parents' royal status to be restored. Instead, he went into the medical field because that's where his heart felt led. During his residency, a pharmaceutical company asked him to shoot a commercial for their product. This became the beginning of a modeling career that took him on other paths. This disappointed his mother, leading her to once tell him that he would become a jack of all trades, but a master of none. That hurt him more than she ever knew.

She preferred that he became something other than a man whose face and body graced the pages of magazines, international television, and the silver screen. The doubt and loss of confidence from his mother permeated his mind, and sometimes a crippling fear would grip him in its ugly jaws. This only compounded the effects of being bullied for his background, since he was the only one with his olive skin tone in a school filled with beautiful alabaster and ivory faces. He learned to make himself small and not voice any of the injustices he endured at the hands of students and teachers alike.

He didn't think he would ever overcome those internal challenges. But he did, and became one of the most sought-after models in the industry. He had been photographed with some of the highest paid women and men in fashion and been part of photo shoots with runway and print icons. That climb took a lot longer than he would have liked, since white males were still paid more than models of color, and women were paid higher than most men. Chaz was grateful for every opportunity sent his way. Though he was still missing that one thing—a soul mate.

His soul did not find peace until he encountered his first love, Rayna, who introduced him to yoga, mantras, and found ways to release many of his demons from the past. The poses, the movements, vocalizing centering mantras and affirmations, created an inner peace that settled him. They had a brief marriage before Susan blasted onto the scene. Somehow professional and personal lines became blurred. So much so, that Rayna gave up on the marriage long before Chaz ever did. Susan was conveniently there to ease the ache in his heart and for a time it seemed that she was a much-needed boost for his career, and everything he wanted to achieve beyond his present milestones.

Chaz regretted moving from one marriage into the next with barely any time to recover. But mostly he felt remorse for how Rayna had suffered because of the break. The only thing he had done right was to choose a woman who wasn't with him because of his money. At first, Susan had more than him. That all changed when he learned to play a few instruments and branched out into singing. Devesh Maharaj had opened the door for East Indian men to go mainstream. Chaz was following in the successful steps of the first of his kind to win a Grammy award.

He needed to take a few months away to do some inner work of his own, deal with the dark parts of him that had been affected by the failure of his recent marriage, and to take time to make things right with Rayna. After this experience with Mandy, he now understood his purpose, his plan, and his destiny. His practice would focus on the mind, body, and spirit connection for healing—using a combination of healing methods steeped in Eastern philosophies.

In hindsight, he realized that Susan was very much in line with his mother. Though she pretended to understand the direction he wanted to go in, every nudge was leading him to let go of the Eastern approach to health and healing, and get back to the industry accepted methods the Western world took stock in.

That would not be his life. He would not be detoured in his purpose ever again. He would create a new international tour to encompass some of the best and the brightest of leaders for change. Spiritual leaders. Spiritual change. Everything started from the inside.

Now he understood, as much as he thought he had grown and invited more balanced relationships into his life, that Susan Keller was more like those women from his earlier modeling days than he realized. Their need centered around what he could do for them. Her need was status and having a man who so many others desired.

He had fallen for her without noticing the shallow person inside. She presented herself as such a professional. Now, he realized she was simply a scared, entitled, and misguided little girl in a woman's body.

But that "little girl" part of her was wreaking way too much havoc.

Chapter 10

"You need to tell him," Christian Vidal warned, sliding a spoonful of gumbo into his mouth. He followed it with a bite of honey-jalapeño cornbread he snagged from a platter in the center of Mandy's dining room table. He had shown up to her humble abode in Pullman, unexpectedly, to check on her at Blair's urging. The two of them—niece and nephew—had been partners in crime growing up. They turned out to be the best thing to happen to Mandy. Since, thanks to an incident with her ex, she had no children of her own, they became her children and she spoiled them way past rotten. And they loved her for it. Karma came around in the fact that they cared for her, especially at the point her life had been in shambles.

Christian was the spitting image of her sister, Melissa, but had the golden skin and thick wavy hair that signaled his Latino heritage. Somehow the nephew she had taken to water parks, played volleyball and taught Spades and Bid Whist, had become a grown man with a graphic arts degree from Columbia, and a few pieces of real estate under his belt, who was handling his business. Not so grown or that much "business" that he could tell her how to run her love life, though.

"No," she said, bypassing his scowling face. "What does that look like, a woman my age, getting pregnant from a one-night stand?"

"One weekend stand," he corrected.

"Whatever," she snapped. "Then coming up to him to tell him that I'm carrying his child?"

Her thoughts flowed back to his generosity in getting a lawyer to represent her before taking her back to the airport. This time, the experience was totally different and she was on her way in a matter of minutes, truly uncovering how much of all of it was related to Susan's words and the minor parts that had already went away with the blood test. She shared parting words to Chaz of resolving any outstanding issues with Susan before he stepped her way. No more drama.

Somehow, those experiences at the hotel and airports didn't explain the phone calls.

They started not long after she finally made it back home. At first, she thought they were all robo calls or someone reaching the wrong number. No matter how many times she blocked the numbers, another phone call would come. Some lasted no more than a second or two. Others involved her saying "hello" a few times. The last one made her blood run cold.

Dead space on the other end made it clear that someone was there, but the breathing sent a shiver of despair through her veins. Death rattles always made the hairs on the back of her neck stand on end. The rhythmic spastic sound of it reminded her of an infant's rattle only instead of bringing attention and smiles, it spoke of the nothingness to come ... of rotting things angling closer for a putrid embrace. Whoever it was, had a soul so ugly they couldn't fathom any idea of leaving Mandy to her modest life.

The feeling that she was being followed came soon after. The air was tinged as if it had already been used. Occasionally the smell left behind was seasoned with musk or grape "vape" juice. Someone was there at the hem of her life, crossing the street with her, caressing her shadow on visits to the doctor or other small errands that she wanted to do alone. Every minute of it stoking her paranoia.

Sometimes it was a creak in the floor or a soft knock from somewhere deep in her home. Even the fresh snap of new paint as a window was thrown open to catch a breeze set her nerves on end. Was it here? Had they found her? Were they going to finish what they started?

She knew better than to chalk it up to nerves or her imagination getting the better of her. When she left Mississippi, the other guards were not too fond of the fact that she had slipped through their fingers. Had they planned her demise even though the judge had found a back-handed way of showing grace, that was actually no grace at all?

She ran a hand over her midsection and frowned. She'd have to be smart about it. She wasn't alone anymore. There were others to consider.

The rattle of Christian's spoon in the bowl pulled her back into the living room. He looked Mandy directly in the eyes. "It looks like a grown ass woman giving him a choice."

"Watch your mouth, nephew."

"I apologize," he said, but didn't sound contrite. "You don't know how he'll respond. Auntie, please don't make the choice for him."

Still, she hesitated. Her trust in men was at an all-time low before Chaz arrived on the scene. Her experience with Kenny repeatedly betraying her trust and manipulating her emotions, taking advantage of her love and her checkbook, had done enough damage for a lifetime. Despite the time and effort she put in to work on that marriage, it eventually became evident that he only wanted her around because he had plans for her paycheck. She might have been a fool, but she was nobody's *damn* fool. She had learned that lesson from her mother at a young age. Some of her sisters never learned, and her mother had done a number on them just like she'd done on Mandy.

"Birth made" family didn't necessarily trump "earth made" family. Her most recent conversation with her sister, Ellena, highlighted the disappointment she felt as Mandy rambled on and on about her troubles. While she knew Ellena was listening, her sister made it clear without saying a word that many of the trials and tribulations people found themselves in were of their own design.

Many talked about going through and being tested, but quickly forgot that part of the test meant owning their stuff and correcting self-sabotaging behaviors.

"It's all about choices," Ellena said over the rim of her cup. "At some point you have to decide what you will and won't put up with. When you're sick and tired enough you'll make a change. Are you Mandy? Are you tired enough yet? I'll move heaven and earth when you are."

Mandy smiled at the memory of the day she had first taken her sister's words to heart.

She ran down to the kitchen and grabbed the garbage bags. Hefty and Glad had been moving baby daddies, cheaters, and deadbeat husbands for decades. They would serve fine for what she had in mind.

His mutters and sputters fell on deaf ears as she gathered his things. With each bit of clothing or possession she threw into the bags, she felt herself become lighter and lighter. All the broken promises, all the pain and betrayal, she bagged it up. With it went the pictures with the fake smiles and the items she purchased for a man who paid more attention to her wallet than the woman he was supposed to love, cherish, honor until death.

"Now that I'm falling in love with you, you're gonna just throw away..."

Mandy put her hand up to silence him. "Oh, now you're in love after how many years?"

"Come on, bae, you know what I mean."

She nodded, slipped a tote bag on her shoulder and locked the front door. "Sadly, I do, but you need to hurry. I packed your things for you. The garbage man is a couple of doors down and I've changed the locks."

"You evil witch."

"Sticks and stones, darling," she taunted. "But damn, I look good in the hat. And a black one at that."

She stared at the hand Christian placed over hers and brought her focus to the present debate. One that was close to Christian's heart because of the way his father had treated him for his entire life.

"He doesn't have children," Christian said in a low tone.

"And there might be a reason for that."

"But you don't *know* if it was him, or his wife, who didn't want them or couldn't have them," he countered, tightening his hold on her hand. "So give him a chance."

"Why are you advocating for him?" she demanded, weary of the discussion that had gone on far longer than she cared to entertain. "You don't even know him."

And neither did she. After the lesson she learned from Kenny, Mandy had put the brakes on with Chaz until he truly sorted his life out and extracted himself, his business, and his interests from his drama queen ex. She recognized the type—clingy, messy, and territorial. Those could make for a dangerous combination to a woman trying to stay under the radar. Chaz was an international public figure, and so was Susan. If she became embroiled in their madness, the Mississippi restitution center could delve a little further into things and find out that Mandy was somewhere she wasn't supposed to be. Being caught breaking parole would change her life even more. And that would not be a good thing.

She had been living under the weight of legal issues for the past two years, starting when a police cruiser tore into her car on a high-speed chase. Even though she couldn't move because of the traffic bottlenecked in front of her, she was unfairly held financially responsible for the resulting damage and relegated to the Mississippi restitution center to work off the incredible debt. The system ran her through that process so fast her head was still spinning and trying to sort it out. Blair and Christian had scraped together the bond money to send the moment she was charged and destined to spend time in that center. Somehow her mother laid hands on the cash and promised to handle the payment. Instead, she and Dorsey, Mandy's sister, pocketed the money. Never sent a dime. By the time the issue was sorted out, the judge stalled on wanting to let her out, tacking on more fees that Blair and Christian had to cover. This delay in her release left her vulnerable to a deadly situation that would change the course of her life.

Between her new criminal record and credit issues caused by Kenny's ruinous ways, she struggled to find a sustainable job. She was forced to take on positions that paid unlivable wages and under conditions that were deplorable. She found that how people treated waitstaff, janitorial staff and day laborers told a lot about who they were. Rich, middle class, white, Black—didn't matter. One of her favorite authors said, "The person who pisses on the floor is not more important than the person who cleans it up." She wished the world would get the memo that everyone had value.

What a person did for a living should not be what defined them. Before that accident and the disastrous end to her imprisonment, she was well on her way to becoming the director of a women's shelter, then owning one of her own. Now she had barely enough to scrape by. Even this house, purchased through grants and forgivable loans which made it affordable, had to be placed in Christian's name.

During the retreat, spending that interlude with Chaz, was the first time she felt … wanted, needed, and dare she say loved. His private journal that somehow ended up in her belongings when they were packing at the Jamaican hotel, had been her life-line to him. The things that he had penned in those pages about the time he spent with her, were the most absolute beautiful things she had ever witnessed in her life. How could he say such loving and compassionate things about her when he didn't really know her. His words penetrated her very soul and made her open in a way that frightened her to the core. This felt a lot like love. This felt a lot like … existing in something more than the pain and the shadows that were like a garment she put on before any stitch of clothing. She wrote the music, but he wrote the lyrics.

Women like her didn't end up with men like him. She and her sisters had better luck with the deadbeat types—like Kenny with his manipulations and money grubbing, or her sister Ellena's ex whose efforts to avoid child support resulted in the death of their four children. She realized that Chaz exhibited none of those ugly qualities, but he was attached to a woman with the ugliest spirit who could make trouble for Mandy. Trouble she could do without.

"I'm a man, Auntie," Christian replied. "I know how it would make *me* feel to be left out of such a huge event. I know how my father abandoning me made me feel. Call Chaz Maharaj."

Chapter 11

"That conniving bitch," Susan screamed and flung her phone across the room. The device slammed against the wall and landed with a thud, partially shattering against the floor of her home office.

Morgan ran inside, scanning the room. "What? Who? What's going on?"

"The hall pass whore," Susan snarled, folding her arms across her bosom. "She's carrying his child."

Morgan inched backward, bumping into the desk before righting herself. "Are you serious?"

"Chaz is so trusting," she spat. "He didn't change the password to his voicemail or emails. I listen in on his messages all the time so I can keep up with what he's about. Deleted that one from her, though."

Morgan's ivory skin flushed crimson. "What?" she gasped. "Susan, you've done some low things in your time, but that is downright cruel. You know he's always wanted a child," she shrieked. "You would deprive him of that?"

Susan didn't bother to feign innocence or try to navigate around Morgan's anger. "If I can't be happy, he can't be happy either."

"You lied to him," Morgan accused, storming across the room until she was face to face with Susan. She stabbed a finger into her chest. "Then you didn't do anything, not one single thing, or any kind of compromise to make it right. None at all. He was honest about his desire upfront. He loved you, and you lied and took away the only thing he wanted."

"Some love that was," she countered, deliberately side-stepping the rest of Morgan's argument. "He fell in love with the first piece of snatch he stuck his cock into."

"A woman *you* chose for him." Morgan shook her head. "A woman you practically laid a path for him to find by your ignorance. You know how Chaz feels about injustice and racism. Especially since he's been a victim of it when he was growing up and during his career. You know others were paid more than he had been—and it was totally unfair. How could you not see how tone deaf you were about using such a racially charged phrase, then responding with meanness to his act of kindness toward a woman you wronged. And after he did whatever it took to make things right, you pushed him at her. What the hell did you expect?"

"She was fat, Black, and ugly," Susan snarled. "How could I believe Mister Perfection would be able to get it up for someone who looked like that?"

Morgan's jaw dropped. "Well, you're a plain Jane, privileged ass, and your spirit is ugly," she said, tilting her head as a dark-eyed gaze narrowed on her. "I can't believe you said that. My grandmother, on my mother's side, guess what she is? So you talking about Amanda McCoy that way is not only disappointing...it's downright sickening."

Susan's heart pounded a mile a minute against her chest. *Would she* lose her best friend over this? And why didn't she know about her family background?

Morgan flinched and grimaced as Susan added, "To fall in love with her was an insult to our marriage."

"Marriage? What marriage?" Morgan shrieked. "You're delusional. You lost him because of your betrayal." She held up her hand to ward off any protest from Susan. "All you had to do was give him one child, Susan. *One*. And you didn't even have to carry it if you didn't want to. He loved you that much."

"Sounds like you wanted him for yourself."

"What if I did, huh?" she retorted, placing a hand on her hip. "I would've at least had the decency to love him as much as he loved me. But you've got it wrong. He only had eyes for you. And I wasn't attracted to him like I am to Noah, so you can't put any of this on me."

Susan stared at a picture of Chaz standing next to her in the Los Angeles Convention Center. The time when they had hosted nearly ten thousand people—all of them experiencing such a wonderful time. The largest event of its kind. They loved Chaz Maharaj. His voice, the way he embraced people, made them feel accepted. "Do you know how many women envied me because he was mine? No way on earth would he choose someone like her over me."

"He did," Morgan shot back. "And he had every right to. She was genuine and real. You have been neither."

"Okay, enough of this vitriol from you," Susan snapped. "Whose side are you on?"

"Mine." Morgan stood straight and pulled back her shoulders. "The side of truth. I don't know what's happened to you in the past, but you've become a bitch lately—a five-star one. All you had to do was choose a surrogate to make him happy. That man bent over backward to keep you. He did everything a man was supposed to do."

"Except love me. Just me. Why wasn't I enough?" she whispered and the pain stabbed her heart all over again. "Why did he need someone else to validate his ego?"

Morgan's jaw dropped a second time. "All these millions of dollars you've accumulated, everything you've built. This legacy." She tapped the top page of a document with the logo Susan had created for her company—one that encompassed several streams of income. "Who are you going to leave that to?"

She shrugged, after mulling that over for a moment. "Charity, of course."

"Is that what *he* wanted?" Morgan countered, and she was beginning to look, sound, and feel like less of a friend with each passing moment.

"No, but—"

"No, that is not what he wanted." She banged her hand on the desk. "The man gave you everything. Everything. Women would kill to be in your shoes—and you blow it all on being so freaking selfish."

"How dare you judge me," Susan screamed, putting some distance between them.

"Lady, the whole world is judging you," Morgan clapped back with a laugh. "With your racist, privileged ass."

Susan blanched, realizing her worst fears were being played out in this scene. "You—"

"You don't even have to say it." Morgan dropped the tablet she carried on the desk. "Consider this conversation my resignation."

"What the hell do you think you're doing," Susan gasped. "You would leave me after everything I've done for you?"

"I'm not even going there. Your meltdown went viral." Morgan glowered at her. "People can see you for who you really are. I certainly did."

"Everyone has a bad day."

"Lady, that wasn't a bad day—that was a bad life," she countered. "You do not appreciate the blessings that have been given to you. You feel *entitled* to them. You say you were empowering women, but you failed to use all that rhetoric to empower yourself. Or at least get the understanding that not appreciating things could have it all taken away. Chaz understood all of that. He, unlike you, was the real deal."

Susan tried to brace herself for the blows lobbed by her best friend. She wiped away a tear. "I can fix this. I'll just have a meeting with him to apologize and give him a kid, then. If that's what it takes to get him back."

"Honey, that train left the station a long time ago." Morgan gathered her things and stuffed them into her backpack. "And you're not listening. Unless you change something within yourself, giving him a child is not going to make him love you again. Lying to him for your entire marriage is what destroyed it. Now, you're aiming to torpedo a chance he has at happiness with the very thing you denied him," Morgan spat, holding her hands out as she backed farther away from Susan until she was at the door. "You make me rethink my whole existence. What does it say about me to be working for someone like you?"

Susan glared at Morgan as she said, "And you can't tell him a thing. There's a nondisclosure agreement."

"Correction, I worked for you five years before all that." Morgan laughed, but there was no humor in the sound. "Your nondisclosure agreements didn't come into force until well after I started. So, unlike everyone else, I don't have one." Moving back into the room, Morgan removed the straps from her shoulders, claimed a seat, then propped her feet on the desk. "Why don't we talk about that severance pay, shall we?"

Chapter 12

"You have a call," Joshua Naples said to Chaz. "A Christian Vidal would like to speak with you."

Somehow, from his attorney's tone, and the timing, Chaz had a feeling this call was about to derail his entire life.

They stood in the dressing room of The Shrine Auditorium, a landmark venue that was the headquarters of the Al Malaikah Temple, a division of the Shriners in Los Angeles. More than six thousand people awaited for him to do the opening session of a week filled with speakers, authors, motivators, yogis and yoginis, health and healing experts—all who came together for one purpose—to effect positive transformation in others so that it flowed out to the rest of the world.

Chaz had changed the direction of his motivational workshops and seminars to make sure they were accessible to all people. Diversity wasn't something he was just now embracing. Time and time again, he insisted on doing things in a way that Susan never understood. Everyone needed healing. Everyone needed to do the inner work. He would not pander to one group or strictly people with money. Inner work and spirituality had nothing to do with ethnic background, status, religion or belief system. It had everything to do with their connection to the Creator; which started with reconnecting with themselves.

In the process of transforming his message and method, some of the people who had been with him for years drifted, while others became downright angry at the influx of people who did not look like them. Maybe they weren't into spirituality at all—just the appearance of being so. Or being and feeling superior to all others. When people can't embrace that all people are deserving of love, abundance, and opportunities, then they are the exact people who need to do that inside work to make them whole. Most didn't realize it, but it wouldn't keep him from trying.

Through it all, he missed Mandy something fierce. He thought he had known what love was all about. Not so. What he felt for Mandy transcended anything he had felt for any woman. And his time with her helped to solidify that this was the right direction for his life. Nearly seven months had passed, and it had taken much too long for him to untangle those last properties from the aftermath of Susan's efforts.

Mandy should be here with him, on the cusp of such a major change in his life.

"Christian is on the line," Joshua hedged, snapping Chaz back to the present. "And it seems urgent."

The tone of his corporate lawyer's voice put Chaz on notice—it was a blend of annoyance and hesitation. Joshua Naples was the lawyer he had hired to handle his personal and corporate business, not be irritated with Chaz's contacts.

"Who is he?" Chaz asked.

"An American. Someone related to Amanda McCoy. Shall I tell him you'll call back?" He smirked before adding, "Or that you won't call at all."

When Chaz narrowed a steady gaze on him, Joshua sighed with frustration and added, "Just close that chapter in your life and move on already. It really will not be in your best interest to be aligned with a woman like that. People already think she destroyed your marriage. She's bad for your image."

"I don't give a damn about that." Chaz gave himself a final look in the mirror, remembering how much energy it had taken not to reach out to Mandy, as she requested when they parted months ago. The properties settled and only then did he reach out for Mandy, but evidently he was too late. He hadn't heard one word back from any of the emails he had his lawyer send out for him.

Even after the intense intimacy and emotion of the weekend they spent together in the airport hotel suite, once the airline security disaster had been resolved, Mandy hadn't felt ready to continue building a relationship with so much uncertainty surrounding his life. Looking back, he couldn't blame her for wanting him to have his entire life together before involving her in it, especially after Susan's meddling that resulted in so much wasted time and grief.

Still, he could kick himself remembering how he let her walk away without insisting on having a way to contact her. Only recently, when the final full division of their business holdings forced Susan to turn over all retreat registration records to him, had he been able to access Mandy's information. He had Joshua do the honors with an explanation and electronic proof that things had ended. She hadn't responded yet, but he would keep trying.

"You should give a damn," Joshua countered, tightening his grip on the phone. "Your brand took a hit with the divorce. Your fan base would rather see you with someone like Susan Keller then Amanda McCoy."

"Then that doesn't say much about them, does it?" Chaz snapped, turning to face him. "So you believe that I should allow *their* preference to rule *my* life?"

"You're right. I don't know what I was thinking," Joshua growled. "If you want to trash your career for a piece of second-rate ass—"

Chaz had Joshua up against the wall in the time it took to blink. "Say that again."

"I am … I am … I …" he stammered.

"Now let me ask you this," Chaz said, noticing that his lawyer hadn't loosened his grip on the phone. "The emails that I asked to be sent to Mandy several weeks ago. What actually happened?"

Joshua inhaled sharply, which meant he was buying time. Chaz gripped his lapel in one fist. "This was long past Susan's expiration date. Lie to me and I swear you'll be thrown off that balcony in no time flat."

"I am … I didn't send them. I never sent them," he confessed, his expression sorrowful as though he wanted Chaz to understand. "You needed to get back with Susan. Adding that woman into the equation was not good for your career."

"Why, because she's Black?"

"Well, if I have to point out the obvious … and a plus-size woman," Joshua yelled. "You're a health, wholeness, and fitness guru. Having a big woman in your bed is a bad look."

"She is voluptuous. And you know what?" Chaz released him so that he slid down and almost landed face first on the floor. "I love every single ounce and inch of her. Hand me the phone."

"I won't let you—"

"You won't let me?" Chaz roared and stepped forward. "I'm about three seconds from destroying my life by ending yours. Give me my damn phone."

Joshua jammed the phone into Chaz's hand.

Shaking with anger, Chaz snatched it, then retrieved the last call. "I don't know why you told me about this new call."

Joshua's skin flushed. "Because he threatened to show up here today if you didn't talk to him."

"And why would he be so determined to contact me at this point in time?"

Joshua averted his gaze and a lick of reddish-brown hair fell over his forehead. "Because I didn't tell you about his other calls."

"You're fired. You know that, right?" He pointed to the door with the cellphone. "Get the hell out of here."

With restrained energy, he punched a button to return the last call that came in. "Chaz Maharaj here. You needed to speak with me?"

"It's about damn time," Christian said on the other end.

"First off," Chaz snapped, eyeing Joshua, who left the room in a hurry. "I'm just hearing that you've tried to reach me before today. So pipe down, fella. What's going on with Mandy that concerns me?"

"Other than the fact that she's carrying your child." His voice dripped with sarcasm as he continued. "Oh, nothing much."

Chapter 13

"So you think this is all a case of pregnant woman jitters?" she asked the officer, trying to keep back a moan of discomfort caused more by the police's slow response to her complaints than by the child trying to make its way into the world two months earlier than normal.

"Ma'am we've looked into your neighbors and your claim that someone has been following you. There is nothing to indicate that such a thing occurred."

Mandy gripped the phone as another contraction hit her, making her double over. This wasn't just a feeling anymore. She saw the vehicles following her. Noticed the scratch marks on the deadbolt on her front door. The gift box filled with dog crap sitting on the top of her car wasn't an illusion.

"Even after everything I've told you about what happened in Jamaica? They held me for questioning as if I killed someone."

"And nothing came of it," he said. "You said yourself that the blood work came back negative. It wasn't your blood on the door. All of that was routine procedure and I don't see anything in the system stating otherwise. I know that must have been a harrowing experience, but there's truly nothing we can do."

She bit down on her lips and tried not to scream. "Never mind. Sorry I bothered you."

"Perhaps if you spoke to your significant other they could allay your fears."

Mandy thumbed the disconnect button and tossed the phone on the chair beside her.

Never complain. That had been her motto all of her life. Never complain because help wasn't coming.

The funny thing about being an ex-offender was that you were always an ex-offender. No matter your crime, even if you paid your dues, you were always considered "less than". Forget the normal employment process. The question was there. Will she commit another crime? Should I make her pay for what happened to me? I can't get the one that stole from me or hurt me, but I can get my pound of flesh in this one. If I do hire them, I can say and do what I want. And they'll be appreciative because they need the job. And they best not ask for anything of their betters.

So what if they did their time? Anything bad that happens to them is cosmic justice, right?

"Right," she whispered through gritted teeth.

Christian came into the room and put a hand on her shoulder. Mandy gripped his hand to give him a comforting squeeze

"Contractions are bad, huh?"

"Closer and closer. I think our little friend is going to make that grand entrance pretty soon." She managed a smile as another wave of pain rippled through her abdomen.

"Auntie, I'm sorry, but you're going to be mighty upset with me."

"Why?" Mandy asked, blowing out a calming breath. The

contractions were coming a little too fast for her to time properly.

Christian's expression grew solemn.

"Why?" she insisted, adjusting herself on the gray sofa which sat across from two royal-blue accent chairs.

"Because I called Chaz Maharaj yesterday."

"You what?" she screeched, and nearly slid to the floor. Instead she gripped his arm. "Please tell me you're joking."

Christian didn't look the least bit repentant. "He had a right to know, Auntie."

"You have a *right* to stay out of my business," she shot back, and popped him upside his head.

Christian ducked, then rested a hand on her shoulder. "You are my business, auntie. I have no intention of leaving for Durabia without making sure you're all right." He issued her a steely glare. "The family wasn't there for you last time. I need to be certain it won't happen again. The baby will need all the support it can get. You, too. Blair sent me here because we didn't want to let you down this time."

"You didn't let me down the first time," she countered. "That was all Dorsey and my mother's doing."

"Blair wanted to come," Christian said. "But they called her into surgery."

Mandy rubbed her bulging belly. "How far out is that ride?"

"They didn't say," he answered, then shifted his gaze to the artwork behind her. "Auntie, please forgive me. There are men who don't want anything to do with their children. Some have gone so far as terminating their parental rights, so they don't have to pay child support. Men who hide in the bathroom at court, so they won't have to say anything to their sons. Those types of men."

Mandy sighed and cupped her hands around his face. "I know that hurt you deeply."

"No worries. My father was an idiot, but it brought about an understanding. Some don't deserve to be fathers. Chaz is different."

"You don't even know him," she countered, letting her hands fall to her distended belly. "I don't think we can wait on this ambulance. The baby is coming."

Christian shook his head. "You can't just ignore—"

"All right, I will call him when I feel—"

His phone vibrated, and he pulled it out and checked the screen. "Your ride to the hospital is here."

"I didn't hear any sirens," she said, her gaze narrowed on him.

Christian simply looked at her until realization kicked in, and she gripped his arms. "Christian, no. Don't open that door. I can't deal with this or anything else right now."

He extracted himself from her hold and crossed the living room.

"Don't open that door," she pleaded.

Christian ignored her command.

Chaz stepped inside and his gaze drifted onto Mandy as he said, "Your chariot awaits."

"You got this?" Christian asked Chaz.

"Yes, I can take it from here."

Christian snatched up his backpack from the space next to her cuddle bench. "Auntie, I have a plane to catch."

Her heart did a tango in her chest. "You're going to leave me with him—alone?"

"It's not like you need a chaperone," Christian said, grinning. "Y'all have already done what gets most people in trouble. And he's not a stranger."

"Well … well, technically he is." She shifted on the sofa and couldn't find a comfortable position.

Christian wiggled his eyebrows playfully. "Well, some parts of you know him better than others. You'll be all right. Gotta go."

He leaned down to kiss her, and she gripped his collar and pulled him closer. "I'm going to whip your narrow ass."

"Auntie, please. Right now, you can't even get up off the sofa." He kissed her cheek and nodded to Chaz. "Save all that ass whipping for him. He looks like he's into that sort of thing."

With a warning glance, Chaz said, "Christian, she can't whip you, but I can."

"Whelp, that's my cue," he said, laughing. "Feel free to name the baby after me."

"Out," they said in unison.

Chaz helped her off the sofa and into his arms, asking, "Why couldn't the ambulance take you?"

"Because they would drive me to the nearest hospital, one where my doctor doesn't practice and one that doesn't have the best reputation on the south side."

"Understood." He gently set her on her feet, then bent to scoop up the prepared bag sitting near the front door. "So where are we going?"

"Advocate Trinity. Dr. Taylor will meet us there."

He carried her outside and settled her into the front seat of his car. Then, he ran to the driver's side, punched the name of the hospital into the GPS and took off.

She exhaled, breathing out for a count of ten. "I tried to contact you."

"Yes, I know," he said, "Stop worrying. Susan's assistant no longer works for her. She gave me a heads up to get a printout of my text messages for the past few months and to change my voicemail and computer passwords. I found out my attorney was also doing some underhanded things right along with my ex-wife. Don't worry." He glanced at Mandy as he accelerated through the yellow light. "Do you know if we're having a boy or a girl?"

"No, I insisted that Dr. Taylor not tell me anything. She said the baby is healthy. That's all that mattered to me."

"Is there anything I need to know—medical history?"

"My age and weight have been the only issue," she said. "But to be honest, this is super early for the baby, so we can expect there might be a few more issues. I just don't know what."

***

Dr. Taylor, a statuesque woman with honey skin, glanced up from her place on the business end of the delivery table and asked, "Are you sure you don't want me to tell you?"

"I'm sure," Mandy said. "This pregnancy was a total surprise. The baby should be one too."

"Right, baby," Dr. Taylor said slowly, shrugging. "Can I at least tell *him*?"

First, Chaz's gaze shot to Mandy, then to the doctor. "No, I'd like to be surprised as well."

"You know, I never agreed with this," Dr. Taylor said. "Which is why I asked to monitor you on a weekly basis."

"Is there something we should know?" Chaz asked with a pointed look at Dr. Taylor.

She grinned, but there was something about the action that didn't seem quite right. Like she knew something important they didn't. "Trust me, it's not a bad thing."

"Then it can wait," he insisted.

"Let's get this party started." Dr. Taylor snapped on the white gloves. "Is the father going with us into the delivery room?"

"I don't—" She glanced over to Chaz, whose expression went blank. "Yes, it's his first child."

His relief was obvious as he clasped her hand. "Thank you, Mandy."

She shared a worried glance with the doctor, who said, "It'll be fine. Phoenix will get him suited up and ready to rock"—she gestured to the nurse, then peered under the blanket and nodded—"because there's a change of plans. We're having this baby right here. It's show time."

No complications existed until the baby came. But Dr. Taylor asked Mandy to keep pushing beyond that first one. Then another one came two minutes behind, and then yet another right after that.

"It's beginning to feel a lot like a clown car around here," Chaz said, grinning while nurses Phoenix and Jennifer cared for the children. Then he peered over Dr. Taylor's shoulder, asking, "Are there any more in there?"

"No, just those three."

"Three? Wait." Mandy gasped, lifting her head. "Excuse me? Did you say three?"

"Yes. Triplets," Dr. Taylor beamed proudly.

Mandy's eyes widened with shock. "I thought you were having me push out the placenta or something! Why didn't you tell me?"

"You insisted you didn't want to know," Dr. Taylor protested.

"I said the sex. I didn't want to know the sex—"

Dr. Taylor passed the last of the three children to the nurse. "Every time I tried, truly tried to mention anything about the baby, you shut it down. Why did you think I insisted on seeing you every week instead of once a month?"

"Because of my age," Mandy mumbled, giving Chaz the evil eye because he chuckled as he held a baby in each arm.

"No, it was because triplets made this even more of a high-risk pregnancy. Your pre-existing condition of overactive ovaries made a multiple birth a very real possibility. We had to be extra careful. Well, that and you already seemed stressed about something or other."

"Oh, my goodness. Three?" Mandy shrieked with a panicked look at Chaz. "What am I going to do with three whole babies?"

"The same as you would for one—love them," he said. "You have support. We will be fine."

Mandy propped herself up on her elbows. "And tie my tubes while you're down there. I cannot have this happen again. I wasn't expecting to be with him or anyone. And now we know the pipes might be rusty, but the damn plumbing still works. Tie them up, put them in a bow and call it a wrap."

The delivery room went silent except for the cries of the babies, then laughter from everyone bounced off the walls.

One of the nurses said, "I'm so glad delivery is over because that would've taken me out."

"And I have it on good authority that the pipes are *not* rusty," Chaz said, smiling down at Mandy. "Thank you very much."

Chapter 14

Several days later, Chaz opened the car door for Mandy to exit. He had rearranged things so that his parents were flying back in early from a trip to India to welcome their first grandchildren. His sister was on a flight right behind them on a long trek from Australia. As soon as he settled Mandy into his home, he would make it to the airport to pick them up.

As she cradled one baby in her arms, she protested, "You can't just kidnap me and take me to a whole new ..."

He repositioned the other two babies in his arms, then led her to the front door of a sprawling house that stole her breath. A woman with a creamy complexion, a pixie cut and a bright smile came to the door.

The heavy oak slab opened to a magnificent foyer that was all bright light with no shadows, just warmth. The open concept floor revealed a stunning kitchen beyond the modern living room with a huge island and breakfast nook. Gleaming hardwood reigned throughout the elegant space.

She stood rooted to the spot, with the baby in her arms, taking in her surroundings. "Wow, this is—"

"Where you'll be staying until you say different," he finished, handing the babies to the other two women who came forward to help.

"I have my own house, Chaz," she said. "And a nursery."

"I know, my love, and that was perfect for *one* child, but there are three." He dipped his chin toward his arms. "And you'll need help and more space."

"Then I'll get another house," she protested, seeming almost panicked.

"But until that time, here, with a chef, a housekeeper, and a nanny, is where you'll call home."

Nita Samms, Karen Burns, and Soneni Pollard, who arrived before them, all appeared at the door, then Karen then accepted the baby from Mandy's arms and passed it to Nita.

Mandy glared at him, her soft brown eyes flashing with fire. "You're not even giving me a choice?"

The two of them were still near the colder side of the threshold because she refused to move past the foyer.

"If you'd like me to take everything and everyone and pack them up and move back to your place, so be it."

Silence descended between them for so long, he didn't think she would answer. He had been inside her place when he tried to prepare for her homecoming. Quaint. Small. Perfect for a single woman. A single woman with three babies? Not so much.

Chaz sighed, realizing that she was not going to give him what he wanted. "Everyone, come and grab your things, we're moving camp."

The women padded toward them. "Seriously?" Karen said. "You mean that dollhouse we just came from?"

"Yes," he said, keeping his gaze on Mandy.

Three other pairs of eyes went to her. She hated to admit "that dollhouse" was almost accurate.

"Chaz, this isn't fair," she huffed. "You could at least ask me. Don't make plans for my life without me."

Duly chastised he said, "Understood."

"Are we staying or going?" Soneni asked. "Because I've got collard greens on the stove, honey fried chicken, garlic mashed potatoes and jalapeño cornbread in the oven." She pointed to the stainless-steel appliances that were the source of all the good scents swirling around.

Mandy blinked a few times, wet her lips, and said, "Well, since you put it that way …"

She glared at Chaz, who was smart enough to adjust his tactic. "Mandy, will you allow me to assist you in these next weeks while we adjust to our new normal?"

"I'll give you six weeks," she replied when several moments had passed. "After I get a clean bill of health from Dr. Taylor, I'm rolling back to my own place."

Sadness filled him for a moment before a plan formulated in his mind. "Fair enough."

"I can take care of myself," she said.

"Understood."

Mandy swept past him and timidly took the stairs one by one as if she knew the layout of the upper floor and where her babies would soon be placed.

"Is she for real?" Soneni said, adjusting her white chef's hat. "All of us in that tiny ass joint?"

"Yes." His gaze included the three women, two of whom had been on his staff for some time. The nanny he had hired recently. "But there's more at work here. Possession is nine-tenths of the law. She is in my domain. I have six weeks for this woman to fall in love with me."

"We've got you," Karen said with a grin, shifting the baby so she could hold her fist out for a pound. Both Soneni and Chaz obliged.

The nanny placed a hand over her heart. "Romance is what I do best." Nita glanced at the stairs, which led to five spacious bedrooms.

"I love a happy ending."

"Not sure about happy," he said, following them all the way to the staircase. "But I'll settle for something close."

Chapter 15

Three weeks later, Chaz came home to find his staff distraught. Mandy had gone out earlier in the day, but hadn't come home and it was now past the children's feedings, which she never missed.

Chaz fought down the initial wave of panic at the thought that she had moved on in her life without him, and set himself to finding a more hopeful explanation for her absence.

His parents and sister had showered her—and the babies—with so much love, she seemed to withdraw a little under all the attention. The same couldn't be said of Chaz and Amanda's relationship. As they had grown more comfortable in the household together over the past few weeks, Chaz and Mandy had delved into deep conversations about family, their goals, and dreams.

Despite their vastly different upbringings, the pair discovered they shared the common burden of disappointment from their mothers. As new parents, this weighed heavy on their hearts and minds. When Mandy had shared her fears about her capacity to be a good mother, especially given the issues with her own, he had told her of his past, including how his mother had sometimes made him feel like success would always be out of reach no matter how much money his accounts had in them.

"Don't get me wrong, my mother was an amazing woman," he said, shifting to stretch his legs out before him. "Doing the best she could, raising a son at a time where prejudice in Great Britain was on the same level as what Black people in America experienced. My mother spoke those words, because she wanted more for me.

"We just have to know that we'll give our children the best that life has to offer. And that we'll be careful not to hurt them the way our parents hurt us. We won't fall prey to using shame or guilt to force them into being what we want them to be, rather than letting them find their way. We also won't allow our fears and generational patterns to put daggers in their hearts."

Mandy locked a gaze with him. "And I want to make sure I never say words that are distorted visions of what manhood or womanhood is like. That won't be our foundation. We are not our parents," Mandy insisted. "We have so much more to go on and are wiser because we understand what drove them and what drives us."

They traded stories of their upbringing and she expressed amazement at his resilience at following his dream of being a healer rather than his mother's of becoming a man who only built a platform to speak out against injustices against women and people of color. The kind his parents experienced in a place that wasn't compassionate to immigrants. One political party—the National Front, the fourth largest one when it came to votes—was against the many people from India, Pakistan, and African countries filtering into the country. Never the Europeans, though. No problem there. Only people who looked like Chaz and his once wealthy parents.

However, Britain had no problem invading India and creating the kind of havoc that changed the fabric of Indian culture. Because of their actions that filtered down and infected some of the locals, Chaz caught hell in school, but put that behind him to excel in his studies. Then he realized he had to scale back that "excellence" because he was hated for an entirely different reason. A sad thing to be forced to make yourself small in order for others to feel "large". In London, he often found himself at the banks of the Thames River when he was feeling overwhelmed. Gazing at the water and reflecting on his life seemed to anchor him, give him a sense of calm and belonging.

Their lives only became better when the family left England and settled in the Bronzeville neighborhood of Chicago—"the Black belt"—a place well known for its nightclubs and dance halls. The jazz, blues, and gospel music that developed with the migration of Southern musicians, attracted scores of diverse listeners and admirers. Like Chaz and his family, Blacks from the south moved to Chicago looking for better opportunities. The first Black owned bank and insurance company was in Bronzeville. Dr. Daniel Hale Williams performed the first open heart surgery at Provident Hospital in the heart of Bronzeville.

Many Black artists, writers, singers, dancers either lived in the same place and building from their childhood. Some jazz greats performed at The Forum, a legendary building on 43rd Street, which also had a "cameo" appearance in a 1970s movie. Music was his father's second love. Weekends were spent listening to Herb Kent, "the Mayor of Bronzeville", spinning oldies, R&B, classics while giving little tidbits of history about music, Chicago, and the artists.

His mother preferred classical music, and her melodious voice was what once lulled Chaz and his sister, Laila, to sleep at night as she tried to soothe an ache she didn't know existed. So, the Maharajs settled in a place where music was timeless, and eventually blended in, and were accepted by the Black community.

Chaz considered the area he now called home the "little neighborhood that could", because it always seemed to be on the edge of recovery. When the area was in the running for the Olympics, a lot of cleaning, clearing, and building went on. Unfortunately, it all stopped when the bid went to another country. Same thing happened when the area was being considered for the Barack Obama Presidential Library. Home and property values went up. Restaurants and other new businesses opened. Some of them closed when the library didn't materialize. But the residents of the community never gave up on rebuilding the area and bringing it back to its former glory. Chaz, who founded several early learning children centers in the area and also created a system of micro-loans for upstart businesses, was doing his part.

Similar to how he felt when walking the Thames River as a teenager, no matter where Chaz went in the world, as far as Denmark, Japan, Switzerland, and as close as California or the east coast, he always came back to Chicago, the south side, Bronzeville, because it was his anchor, it's where he felt most real.

Was there a place that would give Mandy that same feeling of safety and self?

As he thought about her, he remembered how her childhood had shaped her self esteem and expectations, leading her to believe that love didn't happen to people like her. She believed herself damned at birth, coming out between the first five children and the last five. Somehow she, Melissa, and Ellena, had caught the kind of hell that no child should ever experience. Ellena had overcome those obstacles and was now Sheikha of Durabia, a middle eastern country that had fast become the Metropolis of the world. A place where Chaz's mother and father hailed from, and were tossed out of when they fell in love.

Mandy was one of eleven children. Three sets of twins, one set of triplets and two single born children. The two single-born children, and

Mandy, who was one of the twins, had the most tumultuous relationships with their mother, who had committed crimes against her own offspring that would warrant anyone else a place in Cook County Jail. Mandy never understood her mother's motivation and greed—what drove her to do things that were detrimental to her own children, or why the majority of them kept forgiving her.

Mandy had told him that for a as long as she could remember, an unnatural distance existed between Mandy and her mother that could never be crossed. She gave up trying because most times she felt like the child her mother never wanted. She couldn't do anything right in her mother's eyes, and Ruth Hinton made that unfortunate fact known every chance she got. Mandy felt like the black sheep of the family, and she gravitated to other sheep in the meadow who felt the same way—Melissa and Ellena.

She had also shared with him the story of the first time she felt she had the power within herself to stand up and fight for what she needed—the afternoon that she loaded up Kenny's worldly possessions in the finest of garbage bags, and dumped them unceremoniously in the front yard. That decision marked the day she claimed her right to have her own space in the world. The right to a home where she was in full control of the environment and the energy. Where she could find the mental and emotional space to center herself and tune out everyone else's wants for a while. An anchor. And where did Mandy feel most anchored?

"I know where she is," Chaz said, making a U-turn to head toward North Pullman.

"Are you sure?" Nita asked, and the wavering in her voice let him know she was in tears.

"Definitely," he replied. "Don't worry. I'll check in with you all later."

***

With the babies asleep, she took the risk. She had only planned to go to her old house to grab Chaz's journal and some other things while relishing the quiet. Thinking was a hard thing to do in the house with Chaz, the babies, and the staff milling about. They meant well, but she needed some place quiet to think, to relax, relate, and release—at least for a little while. And a moment to reconnect with Chaz through the one thing that held her heart hostage all this time. His belief that she could be loved.

Then the landline rang.

"Pretty little babies, all snug in their pram. Or do they call them strollers in your country? Yes, I believe they do." The crisp clipped British accent sent shivers of unease across her skin.

"Who is this?" she demanded. "What do you want from me?"

"Were you listening when you should have been sleeping?" the voice taunted. "I believe you were. Such a naughty little girl eavesdropping. Had to be sure."

Mandy gripped the phone so tight a nail cut into her skin. "I don't know anything."

"Found the blood on the doorway, didn't they? Can you keep a secret? There was more... lots more. Imagine if it followed you home. It gets into everything ... Everything."

"Please leave me alone ..."

"Can you keep a secret? I know you can. With your past ... I'm sure you are an expert at keeping secrets."

"What do you want?" she asked, this time her words sounded more like a plea, trying to still the galloping of her heart against her chest. "I don't have any money."

"Eye for an eye... tooth for a tooth... a life for a life?" the sing-song quality of the voice on the other end dissolved into a cackle as the line went dead.

The muscles in Mandy's legs went slack as the receiver slipped from her hand and bounced across the floor.

* * *

Three hours later, she had forced herself from the chair to rummage through the closet and found a long-forgotten baby blanket she had started crocheting forever ago. One blanket, not three. This was before there were three to speak of. The soft blues and yellows moving through her fingers began to grow into a granny square as she felt the stress gradually leaving her body. With every expanding round, she sorted through her memories trying to put a name or a face to the British accent on the phone and what they said. She remembered the biblical scripture, but the words were out of context.

The thoughts ran laps in her mind, thinking of every possible scenario when a knock at the door snatched her attention.

Mandy opened the door and gasped when she looked out at Chaz. "How did you know where to find me?"

"Wild guess."

Her eyes widened to the size of saucers. "You don't have like a tracker on me or anything like that, do you?"

"Your nephew does—not a tracker, but he threatened to separate a certain body part if I wasn't handling my business."

She frowned. "What business?"

"You," he said, as though she should have known that already. "May I come in?"

"Yes, sure," she answered, stepping aside to allow him inside. He placed his coat on the rack then perched on the micro suede cuddle bench, settled in, and waited. Silent moments ticked by before he picked up the blanket in progress and smiled. "I didn't know you crocheted."

"Learned when I was a child. Something about the rhythm of it and the feel of the yarn," she said, taking a seat on the sofa across from him. "The idea that you could fashion something beautiful out of nothing. I figured if I could make something beautiful, maybe it would combat the darkness. Maybe I wouldn't feel so lost." Mandy leaned forward, extracted the material from his hands, and worked another round of the soft yarn through the loops.

Time ticked by and he wondered if she would open up to him again.

"You aren't lost, Mandy. I found you. Your nephew, your niece, your sisters. I want to help… we all want to—"

Finally, she sighed and looked at him. "How can I have so much help and still feel this way?"

"What do you mean?"

"I wasn't ready. Not for you. Not for them," she confessed. "Whether it was one, or two, or whatever." Her eyes were moist with tears. "What if I get it wrong? I heard what you said, but what if I mess them up, the same way my mother messed us up? And I have girls. *Two girls*. The world is not a safe place for them. Never safe. I brought three little people into such an ugly, horrible world. What the hell was I thinking?"

Chaz left the cuddle bench and settled in a spot next to her on the sofa, brushing her tears away with his fingertips. "Can I tell you what I'm thinking? Will you listen to what I have to say?"

Mandy nodded, and he gently gathered her into his arms, the first time he had done so since she came to live with him. She was keeping that distance at their home to the point that they still had separate bedrooms.

She didn't resist.

He had been pacing things, waiting for her to see the advantages that love could offer; that a life with him could offer.

"I'm thinking that God knew that at some point," Chaz began. "These three beautiful beings would need the best parents possible and he loaned them to us for a little while," he whispered. "Because he knew that we, in whatever capacity available to us, would do everything in our power to keep them safe." He pressed a kiss to her temple and she curled into him, evidently enjoying the comfort as much as he did. "The one thing I do know, is that for years I wanted a child—first children, then it trickled down to one—just one—with a woman I believed was my forever mate.

"One incident—well, a series of small incidents, showed me how untrue that was. That's why she is no longer part of my life. But the Universe heard my request and placed you in the most precarious of circumstances for you to be in my path." He stroked her hair. "That one night—actually, one amazing weekend with you—brought an answer to the only two prayers I've had for years. One, for a woman who would love me unconditionally. It couldn't have happened any other way. Because who I thought was for me would not be the answer to the other part of my prayer. Two, for the children that I would have to be healthy, happy, and complete. That they would not be exposed to the struggles and pain that their parents experienced." He used a fingertip to tilt her chin upward so her eyes met his. "I have no doubt in my mind that we are the right parents for our three children."

"You really think so?"

"I know so, honey," he answered. "These children were conceived in love and compassion. The world might be a scary place, but we love them, and we will do the absolute best that we can."

Chaz held her for a while, then scanned the Hiram Harris artwork, angel figurines, and other décor in her living room. A place bursting with color, but sadness had settled here—a vibe he could never shake, no matter how many times he came.

"This is the house of sorrows," he whispered directly against her ear. "When you leave this place, you will leave your tears here, your pain here, your sorrows here, your doubts here, the poverty here, the lack and limitation—it all stays here. When you cross the threshold, embrace the possibility of happiness, the possibility of joy, the possibility of love."

Chaz kissed her deeply, taking his time, and the world was all right with him. "This will be another point for the win column. Life zero—Mandy one. Then, and only then, will it enter your mind that loving me and having a family was meant to happen. Those children were already written in the stars." He embraced her again, then pulled out of her grip. "I will leave you to handle this ... darkness part of your business, because by your actions you asked for space and I'm going to respect that."

He left the house, so he wouldn't witness the savage beauty of her pain; something she said seemed to follow her all the days of her life. Releasing it meant she had to experience and walk through the valley of condition because that was all she knew. Then, she would be ready to know something else. Something like ... loving him.

Chaz slipped into the driver's seat, inhaled, then relaxed and released nine times until he felt a certain balance. The flurries of snow floated around him, and a chill would follow, but he planned to wait right here, no matter how long it took.

He turned on the car to get a little heat, reminiscing on the joys of fatherhood, something he never thought he would experience in this lifetime. Tara, Saira, and Malik were amazing little beings. They were being spoiled rotten by Soneni, Karen, and Nita.

Mandy joked that in a minute the babies wouldn't know who to call mother. She shared her fears sometimes, a snippet of what was holding her hostage. He was silent when necessary, supportive where he needed to be, but still ... not enough where she felt comfortable enough to let her guard down.

Chaz sighed, concerned by the fact that Mandy wouldn't open up to him. Not like she had in Jamaica. Certainly not like she did in Jackson. If she wouldn't let him in, it might only be a matter of time before she left him altogether.

Chapter 16

Mandy lay on the bed, trying to find a sense of calm. Every time she thought of Chaz, and that maybe, just maybe they could be something more, the experiences from that night in Mississippi came to the forefront. Even if she *could* trust Chaz not to betray her faith in him, faith that had been smashed to pieces in her first marriage, could she ever let go of the horrific images in her head of that awful night and her deadly actions?

She had packed her minimal amount of things, then had been removed from the hotel where she was housed with the other women who would be let out during the day to work in local restaurants. The three deputies escorted her to a place that did not look anything like the processing center she'd been through on the way into the system. Instead, they guided her into a hotel room to await transport.

Only then did she find out that the judge had added a requirement that wasn't in any of the paperwork. She was set to "service" two of the men who played poker with the judge every week. Other women from the center had been brought in as well.

Mandy only learned of the true intent of this desired outcome of her evening by hearing snatches of conversation among the men. Those guards decided they wanted a piece of the action first, and were prepared to give her a going away present before handing her off to the judge's poker buddies. All part of the nefarious design of a legal system so rife with corruption, Satan already had their names written in his date book. That night, no one got what they wanted. Only three people got what they deserved.

The other women watched in shock as Mandy fought the two officers restraining her, while the third tried to have his way with her. To this day, she didn't know where or how she got the strength to yank the gun from the guard's holster, shoot that man and smash another in the face. Then she made the third eternally sorry he tried to make her give up what wasn't his to take.

The retaliation was swift, but no one wanted the true details to come out. After a bench trial where the judge refused to allow her to have outside counsel or anyone to speak on her behalf, in an effort to keep the details from going public, Mandy was shuttled out of the city and back home under a non-disclosure agreement and restricted parole. This also came with the stipulation that she pay three million dollars over a stretch of several years as restitution to the families of the officers she had killed and the one she had maimed. She was grateful for her freedom and it was mostly because of Blair and Christian, but the cost she was paying as part of a back-door deal came at an unreasonably high price which meant that her bank accounts were constantly drained. That was the plan all along. She was in a prison of another making.

That trip to Jamaica was the only thing she had done for herself in years. Despite all the chaos at the airport, the wonderful aspects of time she spent there would forever be etched in her mind.

Nineteen minutes later, she called Chaz. He answered on the first ring. "Yes, Mandy?"

"Why are you still outside?" she questioned. "It's cold out there."

"Because the moment you make up your mind it's time to come home and explore the possibilities that exist in your new life, and also decide you will allow a little space in your heart for me to court you properly, I don't want you to have to wait."

Mandy was silent, thinking about his words; thinking about every wonderful thing he had done since he had come back into her life. Could she trust him with her heart? With her history? Trust was a hard thing to come by. But when he prompted her to answer by calling her name, she said, "Come and get me."

* * *

Nita, Karen, and Soneni rushed toward Mandy and gathered her in their arms for a group hug.

"Oh, thank God," Nita sighed. "How could we have told him we lost track of the woman he loves?"

The chef cringed. The housekeeper gasped.

The nanny glanced over Mandy's shoulder and froze. "Did I say that out loud?"

No one spoke. No one moved.

Chaz's expression went from shocked to resigned.

"Love?" Mandy tossed out, her face a mask of concern.

"I need the room, please," Chaz said.

"You were gone so long." Nita scanned everyone's panicked faces, as she said, "I just assumed that you told her—"

"The room, please," he insisted.

Nita inched backward and landed against Soneni and Karen. "My apologies."

"No worries," he assured her, then gestured for the others to take her with them.

"You're not going to fire me for giving it all away, are you?"

"Come on, loose lips," Soneni said, draping an arm around Nita's shoulder to guide her toward the stairs leading to the second landing. "Let's find another ship for you to sink."

The moment the three of them cleared the area, Mandy whirled to face him. "Love? They knew it and I didn't. *Love*?"

"From day one, in Jamaica," he confessed, closing the distance between them. "The moment you chose peace over making a scene, even when Susan took such pains to embarrass you, your strength touched my heart. Then after all the success you had with embracing yoga and some of the techniques, I was so moved by your willingness to try."

The experience went a long way to reminding him that this was his purpose. Healing on this level—not the mechanics of medicine—was what he should truly be about.

Mandy searched his eyes.

"Then when you said I don't bring receipts, I bring invoices …"

"Yes, that was pretty good," she said, laughing.

"So yes. I am hoping that we will find our way to love." He pulled her into his arms. "Welcome home, honey. Welcome to your new life."

Chapter 17

Susan sauntered inside the luxurious Bronzeville home, and past Mandy's housekeeper as she took a good look around. From what Chaz told Mandy, several months had passed since he'd spoken to Susan. Only one final piece of business was left to contend with. Susan had filed paperwork to trademark *his name* to keep him from using it in his new business ventures.

Mandy finished feeding her youngest, then moved off the sofa and handed her to Karen, who gave Susan the evil eye. "I'll just be a minute, then I'll feed my son."

Wearing a loose white pantsuit under an artic fox fur, Susan was the epitome of elegance. That paled by the fact that her eyes shone with malice as she glided across the room, picking up a framed photo of the triplets from above the fireplace. "So, you managed to worm your way into his life and take him from me."

"He wasn't trying to stay in any kind of marriage with you." Mandy's tone was cool as she went to the front door and held it open, signaling that she didn't want the woman to stay. "You're delusional if you thought the two of you were going to get back together."

"You don't know that," Susan snarled, placing the photo back on the fireplace mantel.

Keeping her composure, Mandy said, "Paper trails don't lie."

"So, you whelp three pups and he's supposed to fall in love with you?" Susan's tone was filled with disdain. "Marry you?"

Mandy had battled for weeks not to fall in love with Chaz and lose herself the way she had with her first husband.

Chaz had given her space and they still slept in separate rooms until she said they could move forward. The only emotional barrier between them was that she'd been reluctant to tell him of her history in Mississippi. She was losing the fight, and he was winning a space in her heart. But trusting him after what the men in her family had done; what her husband had done, what the judge had done, was challenging. The fear that Chaz would hurt her also ruled her mind and served to keep her guard up.

"He doesn't have to marry me." Mandy circled Susan, who tipped her chin into the air. "How are you going to be upset when you were the one pushing him in my direction? Didn't you give him a … hall pass? And didn't you lie about all those times you did away with his children?" She faced Susan, thumbing toward the exit. "You're going to have to come back later if you want to speak with Chaz. He won't be here until after nine. But I will tell him you stopped by."

"I can simply wait until he returns," she said, gesturing to the sectional in the center of the living room as the spot she intended to hold court.

Karen peered around the corner to look in on them. She gestured to her watch to remind Mandy she needed to get on with feeding the babies.

Standing taller, Mandy let a smile come to her lips. "Actually, I'm quite busy here with three newborns that need my attention and I don't have time to entertain unwanted guests." She pointed to the door. "Like I said, you can come back later. Better yet? I'll have him call you. Can't have negative influence around my children, you understand. See to it you close the door behind you."

After a silent battle of wills, Susan backed down and stormed out.

* * *

Mandy closed the door behind Susan and rested against the wall. She thought she'd had a bad turn with her ex, but Susan was another thing entirely. How had Chaz not seen who she really was?

She was one to talk. She had witnessed a change in Kenny but couldn't understand what had caused the transformation. Their marriage failed because of money, but when Kenny realized he'd really lost her he resorted to the tool of "big men" throughout history.

The first slap was delivered over breakfast because the eggs were too runny. The twelfth was over an Italian Fiesta Pizza order he said was wrong, even though she picked up *exactly* what he asked for.

If she was honest with herself, the issues between them actually began on the first day of their marriage and didn't get better with time.

Kenny was too drunk to make love to her on their wedding night. After he pulled that "let's make it special and wait until we're married" mess. That should've been a tip off. Instead, she had believed the gesture was romantic and he cherished her enough to wait.

When she reached for him, he cringed then pulled the blanket up on his shoulder and passed completely out. Later, after this happened too many times, she figured out she should've taken Kenny for a test drive.

Then she would've known that the "long black limousine" he swore up and down he had, was actually a "Mini Cooper" that couldn't pull up to anyone's bumper.

Another slap came over a dinner she'd fixed for the anniversary of the day they met. She demanded to know why he smelled more like Donna Karan than Miller Genuine Draft, and spent the remainder of the evening trying to scrub the blood stains out of her new shirt while nursing a lip that could circle the block and still never run back to its normal place on her face.

Bloody noses meant flowers or candy. A puppy had been thrown in there somewhere, but she gave it to one of her neighbor's children after Kenny threatened to throw it in the oven for messing on the carpet. Broken bones and a miscarriage meant expensive trinkets bought with bill money. Clothing purchased as gifts never fit and earned another fist if a complaint came instead of a thank you. After all, one mustn't be seen as being ungrateful or unappreciative.

The first beating with a belt was embarrassing. The ninety-first, well, it was just another one of those things a long-suffering wife had to deal with. Her mother certainly did. Going to the family was out unless she wanted to be the topic of conversation when she wasn't in the room.

No, as crazy as it sounded, the punches were easier. Get him mad enough to start the cycle that always ended with her cowering on the floor. Whatever it took to keep the peace, even if it meant giving a piece. Not that he wanted that anyway.

On the off chance he did want sex, it had been painful and degrading. The one time she asked him to turn out the lights he said, "Why? Won't hide the fact of who you are."

Two drops of blood on her new furniture slipcover ended all of that. Well, that and a phone call from her sister Ellena.

"You tired yet? Are you finished being his punching bag? Because I can say it all day, but until you've had enough ... "

Mandy knew how to survive, and do that "marriage-ego-compromise-it's my fault" dance—because she signed up for this, right? She took vows before God—death do them part and all that. Marriages had their volatile moments. Her grandmother's did. Her mother's did. That's just how things went. She felt that way until the night he tried to force himself on her. She wasn't having it—or him.

She managed to get him off her and hide out in the bathroom, getting herself and her thoughts together. She walked into the kitchen to grab her purse and cell to make the call for Ellena and Melissa to come and scoop her up. She wouldn't fight with him to leave. No, she would do the honors—and he could keep every damn thing. She was done. She was done, done!

While she waited for them to arrive, she cleared the last remnants of dinner.

Kenny stuck out a leg and she went sprawling. Their empty dinner plates shattered on the floor as the silverware scattered.

"Damn you're clumsy." He snickered and something ugly crawled into her soul. "All that ass hitting the floor worse than an earthqua—"

Mandy grabbed the knife, blurred the distance between them with eight quick steps, and drove it through his foot and tethered him to the floor.

She scrambled back against the wall, clutching her blood-slicked hand against her bosom.

"You bi—"

"Let bitch roll off your tongue," Mandy warned, bracing herself as an uncharacteristic strength came over her. "And you won't be using your other foot either."

He screamed as he extracted the knife with a great heave, then hobble-walked into the living room. She inched further across the kitchen to the threshold and watched as he snatched her favorite pink and purple granny square afghan from the back of the sofa and wrapped it around his wounded foot.

She had married into that type of madness. She grew up with sisters who had to protect themselves because mothers and grandmothers couldn't keep them safe from men who saw them as easy prey.

And Chaz wanted her to trust him? After men who were supposed to love her didn't respect her, or her right to make her own choices?

No.

Give them enough alcohol and the thing that lived behind their eyes awakened. On a regular, it was small and mean, with cheap beer or whiskey coming through the pores. Sometimes the screams were enough.... sometimes it inspired them...egged them on.

No.

No alcohol? No problem.

Sometimes they just grew tired. Sometimes the 'man' was keeping them down, or whatever made them small and afraid, but was somehow her fault.

No.

Broken bones and bruises made it clear she knew how to earn her keep. She had had her fill of men exercising options they didn't have. She'd rather be alone than stay somewhere unhappy. Her children deserved better. She deserved better.

Men were supposed to be the head of the household, the spiritual head. How was that possible when their insecurities seemed to pool into their fists as they sucked the life out of bank accounts, self-esteem, and whatever else a woman had.

Men failed, and damned if they weren't good at it, and somehow, someway, it was always "her" fault. Women paid with their hopes, dreams, bodies and minds. They paid even when the debt wasn't one they owed.

Imagine men being so afraid of the innate power of a woman that they killed to silence it.

No, she was done. She didn't have time for forever.

She would not … could not fall for it again. No way. No how.

Chapter 18

"You could file an alienation of affection lawsuit against her," Monyette Holiday said, laying down her silver pen. Her dark-brown eyes, mahogany skin, and tamed microbraids presented a picture of confidence and efficiency. As did her cream-and-brown office furnishings.

Susan looked up from the article in her hand, still miffed about her episode with Mandy. She had made a beeline straight to a lawyer recommended by Sheila Washington, her lawyer in California, because she had no one else to confide in.

She was missing Morgan something awful. But her former best friend had made good on keeping her distance and not taking any of Susan's calls. Even though all she wanted to do was apologize. Susan specifically requested a Black lawyer to handle this nasty piece of business. It irked her to no end that a woman who was on the poor end of the spectrum and had nothing going for her, had somehow made off with Susan's knight in shining armor. "So those types of things still exist?"

"In some states, yes," Monyette answered, handing over a file.

"The wife can sue the mistress if she was the cause of the marriage dissipating."

"But she wasn't," Susan admitted. "She was after."

"Yes, but thanks to the judge holding the paperwork in that manner, you were 'possibly' reconciling. That's all that matters."

"But we won't win if they find out the dates and everything doesn't line up."

Monyette shrugged. "You'll succeed in discrediting her and it'll be enough to get Chaz's attention to make a nuisance go away."

Susan's heart plummeted, thinking of everything that had transpired. If only that woman hadn't come to the retreat. If only Chaz hadn't redirected his attention to a straggler. If only he … "The man hates me."

"He doesn't hate you," Monyette assured. "And all he needs is a nudge in the right direction. Trust me, he'll come back to you eventually. The two of you made sense. This new woman is scraping the bottom. You made more money together. Well, *you* did once he became part of the equation."

She slid another document in front of Susan, who glanced at the caption on the lawsuit.

"So, you really think this is really the way to go?"

"Yes, let's put her ass on blast as a homewrecker," Monyette said, grinning. "See what shakes out."

Susan sighed. "Let me think on it a few days."

* * *

"Glad you could make it in on such short notice," Monyette said, gesturing for Susan to take a seat across from her in the boardroom a few days later. "I received an envelope from someone who said you couldn't possibly have met Amanda McCoy in Jamaica. She's on parole."

"Parole?" Susan's heart leaped as she slid the letter out and scanned the contents. "Who sent it?"

"The wife of the man Amanda killed."

Susan's head whipped up as she squeaked, "Killed?" *Amanda McCoy is a killer?*

"Evidently, Amanda McCoy went to jail for not being able to pay for a squad car that was damaged. She ended up in one of those infamous restitution centers in Mississippi. She was set to be released after the money finally came through, but the night before they brought her for processing, three guards tried to sexually assault her. She killed them before they succeeded."

"Them?" Susan croaked.

Monyette scanned the screen. "Yes, well, only two of 'em."

"Only?"

"She shot one of them, and the other is permanently blind in one eye. The third, she jammed the gun his nose and it collapsed. He died from suffocation right there on the scene."

Susan sat back in the seat and swallowed hard. "What a horrible experience."

The lawyer nodded, waiting, but scanned the documents regarding Mandy's case again.

"On second thought," Susan said, exhaling a long slow breath as her heart went out to Mandy. But only for a moment. "Maybe we should rethink this lawsuit. She seems … dangerous."

"And she might already be pissed off by the article that slander rag did on her and Chaz, so what's the difference," Monyette countered.

Moments passed as Susan mulled over her options. The more she thought about losing Chaz, that this woman came out of nowhere and derailed her business, the anger filled her all over again. "File the suit," Susan said as she signed the engagement letter she had placed on the top of all the documents along with the hefty retainer she required. "No way does she get to win. My husband, those children. She does not get to walk off with everything. She doesn't get to have my life."

"Are you sure?" Monyette asked, and for the first time her lawyer's voice didn't instill confidence.

"Yes."

"We'll have to file it in Mississippi," Monyette warned, placing the letter back into the file.

"But we lived in California."

"Yes, you have a place there, but your roots and family are in Mississippi. His main place of residence is in Bronzeville. They don't have alienation of affection laws in California or Chicago. And even though their affair happened in Mississippi, you'll have to actually have a residence there to file the case. And it'll mean we have to engage a local lawyer as well." Monyette slid the document into a file. "We're more likely to get a favorable judge there in Mississippi."

"Well, chop chop," Susan said, grinning. "Let's buy me a house down there near my family. And while we're at it, let's make sure the judge in her current case gets wind of it. Parole violation, right? Problem solved."

Chapter 19

Chaz left his office when the doorbell rang, quick-stepped through the kitchen, gave a high five to Soneni who was whipping out another scrumptious dinner, then opened the door to find three beefy officers on the other side.

"We have a warrant for Amanda McCoy's arrest." They shoved the document into his chest.

He barely caught it before it landed on the floor. "No, this can't be happening." Frowning, he looked up from the warrant. "But this is for a case in Mississippi."

"Yes, she's wanted on a parole violation," one of the officers said.

"Parole?" Chaz shook his head. "What the hell? This can't be right."

On silent feet, Mandy came downstairs and stood at his side. She glanced at the officers, closed her eyes, and inhaled deeply.

"What's this about? What do I have to do?" He gripped her shoulders and met her eyes. "Honey, tell me."

"There's nothing you can do," she whispered with a wary glance at the men crowding their doorway. "Can you give me a minute, please?"

One guard, whose badge read Rob Walker, said, "Only a minute, ma'am."

"Parole violation?" he asked, mystified.

Mandy nodded. "Your retreat was in Jamaica," she explained, placing a velvet jewelry bag in his hands.

A note of frustration entered his voice. "Yes, and what does that have to do with any of this?"

"I had permission to leave, but they wanted more money," she said in hushed tones so only he could hear. "They *always* want more money. So, I had to choose between the retreat and hoping that they didn't find out. Guess which one I chose?" Mandy's gaze lowered to the hardwood floor for a moment. "When I made it back, I was supposed to pay them, but after I paid for the change fees for the flights, and then another flight home from when I finally made it into the States, I didn't have anything left. By the time I had the money, if I paid it, there would have been too many questions because I had already put in that the trip was for a certain date. I figured that if they hadn't said anything ..."

"I can pay the money," Chaz said, facing the men. "Just let her go. Here—" He reached for his wallet and pulled out several hundred-dollar bills and a credit card. "I have the money."

"That's not how it works, pal," Absalom Williams, the tallest of the three warned. "We're going to need you to back up."

"Damn, you got it like that," the other officer said, peering into Chaz's wallet. "Just walking around with stacks and whatnot."

"Honey, I'm going to get the best lawyers. She just had children—three of them," Chaz implored, alarmed when one man pulled out handcuffs. "How can you just take her away like this?" Chaz asked. "Do you have to put her in those?"

The three men shared a glance before one said, "She killed two guards and blinded a third one. She's considered dangerous. Even unarmed.

There are people serving life sentences for far less. She must've had a damn good lawyer."

Chaz winced, still uncertain as to what had happened to her in Mississippi and though he had the resources to find out, he preferred that the story come directly from her. The fact that she hadn't felt comfortable enough to share, showed how much distance still existed between trust and love.

"I don't even know how they let her out on parole in the first place," the second officer mumbled. "And for two officers at that."

Chaz absorbed that information and moved in to say something else, but the officer who now gripped Mandy's upper arm said, "Back up, or you'll be going in with her."

"Call Christian and Blair," Mandy said to Chaz. "They'll give you all the information you need."

Still in shock, Chaz tried to unravel the scene playing out in front of him. The men escorted Mandy to the vehicle and helped her inside. Fury stirred low in his belly and exploded in his chest. After that disgusting article in the paper, he should have known it was the first of many arrows shot at them. This was too sudden and had Susan's hands all over it. He pulled out his phone. First, he'd talk to Mandy's relatives.

Then, he'd deal with Susan Keller.

Chapter 20

"New fish."

The raucous call came from one of the inmates.

Mandy walked the long corridor until she made it to the cell. The officers strip-searched her and outfitted her in one of the most uncomfortable garments to wear before escorting her into the belly of the cell block. All the while, Mandy fumed knowing that Susan's hatchet job in that scandal rag had done more damage than she could imagine. That woman should have been the one on meds because she certainly had it in for Chaz, and Mandy by default.

This entry into prison life was drastically different than what she experienced as part of her restitution center stint. There, the women were imprisoned in low budget hotels that were situated close to the restaurants where they had designated assignments. Those hotels were like a palace compared to this place.

She ignored the burst of sounds—debates, rapping, singing, loud conversations, that came from every corner of the units. After she scanned the range of smirking, solemn, and expectant faces in the area,

Mandy realized speaking would be the polite thing to do.

"Y'all got company," Officer Williams said.

"Good Evening," Mandy said.

"Good Evening," one almond-eyed Latina taunted with a laugh. "All proper and everything."

Everyone laughed, but Mandy found no humor in her current situation.

Mandy's cell was smaller than her bathroom back home. Concrete from top to bottom, including the floor. The cell contained a toilet, sink, and two metal beds with mattresses so thin they were almost non-existent. Privacy was a thing of the past. An underlying smell of urine and musk permeated the air from too many bodies being cramped in such a small space. She didn't know how she would survive here.

"Ten minutes 'til count," blared over the PA system in a droll, bored voice that didn't spur anyone to action.

"You heard the man," Officer Williams said. "And you know the drill. Make sure she learns fast. She already has a few things working against her."

"Yeah, yeah, yeah," a spiky-haired blonde muttered, turning her back on the group. "On the bunks in plain sight. Like we haven't heard that every single day for the past few years."

"Speak for yourself," a petite Asian said, "I've been here a lot longer."

"Yes, like when Moses parted the Red Sea."

Laughter filled the cell.

"Where should I sleep?" Mandy asked, pulling the itchy wool blanket close to her chest.

"With me, anytime," another suggested. "The name's Nikki."

Even more laughter echoed around Mandy and she braced herself for other snide remarks.

"Top bunk. Over there," a tall, statuesque woman said. She had a commanding presence and everyone stepped aside to let her come to the front. Obviously, the leader of the pack.

"Thank you." Mandy moved forward, but no one parted to let her pass. "Excuse me."

Still no one moved.

"Cut it out, y'all," the woman said.

Only then did the other three shift so Mandy could maneuver around them.

"Thank you." She placed her meager belongings on the top bunk, then struggled to climb up on the bed.

"It'll take a minute," the blonde woman said. "But you'll be a pro in no time."

Mandy gave her a half-smile, then stretched out on the hard cot.

"Look at her," someone teased. "A real prima donna already."

"Leave her alone," the leader warned. "You know how it is when they first come." She moved forward until she stood next to Mandy's bed. "They're only going to give you a minute to adjust. I know you're feeling sorry for yourself right now, but when count hits or the chow bell rings, you gotta move. When the work bell rings, you gotta leave. You won't be able to stay here. Got it?"

Mandy sat up. "Yes ma'am."

"It's Rae." She pointed to the Asian woman and said, "That's Linda." Gesturing to the blonde, she added, "Nikki. The one with all of the mouth is Sabrina."

"Thank you." She extended her hand to Rae. "I'm Mandy."

Rae looked at the hand, then back at Mandy before accepting it. "What are you in for?"

Voices trickled to a hum, then everyone in the cell went quiet.

"Parole violation," she whispered, wishing she could disappear into the concrete.

Rae tilted her head and peered at her. "No, I mean, what are you *really* in here for?"

Mandy thought putting them on notice was the way to go. "I killed two men. Prison guards."

"Oh man," Rae sighed and put a hand over her heart. "They're gonna make your life absolute hell."

Chapter 21

"Hey, I brought along some reinforcements," Christian said, gesturing for the other men to follow him inside Chaz's home. "My Aunt Ellena says these guys are the best. How are you holding up?"

"I'm losing my fucking mind," Chaz growled, pacing the marble floor in front of the fireplace. "Knowing she's in a place like that and doesn't deserve it."

The seven men settled in the seats around the living room, facing him.

"They just took her, Christian." He gestured to the boxes. "And the lawyers I've hired keep getting stonewalled. They needed local counsel, but every last one of them wanted to play ball with prosecutors who aren't used to people making waves."

Chaz handed Christian a folder. "They have an airtight legal machine down there and no one wants to take them on. What they did to Mandy those years ago, putting her in jail for such a small nonviolent offense, is practically non-existent in other states."

Then he passed them a banker's box filled with documents. "I've done my research. They have been getting away with this for years. This is a money pipeline for rich white men. Cheap forced labor, arresting people with little or no cause, denying them their legal rights without much recourse because everyone who matters is in their pockets." He threw up his hands in disgust. "Some people have committed crimes and yes, they deserve to be behind bars. But the disparity between sentences means this whole thing is nothing more than thinly disguised slavery."

"What's that?" Christian asked, nodding towards the purple velvet jewelry bag Mandy had given to Chaz when the officers came for her.

"My journal," he replied. "I thought I lost it on the island, but Mandy had it all those months we were apart." He paused and met Christian's gaze. "She's going to spend the rest of her life in there if I don't get her out somehow."

Christian gestured to the men sitting around them. "This is Khalil Germaine Maharaj, the founder of The Castle. Daron Kincaid who's a tech guru and inventor. Dro Reyes, a fixer. Shaz Bostwick, who's an immigration lawyer, but has a foundation for helping mothers who find themselves in trouble with the law. Vikkas Maharaj is also a lawyer, but it's on the international side. And Jai Maharaj is a medical doctor. They are all managing members of The Castle—an organization that's built on humanitarian efforts. I think they can help us out."

Chaz angled his head toward the men. "Did you say Maharaj?"

"Yes," Christian answered, his gaze focused on Chaz. "Why?"

He extended his hand to the man named Khalil who had silky salt and pepper hair, and an olive complexion that matched his own. "Chaz Maharaj."

Christian's gaze panned across all the Maharaj men, whose features were interestingly similar. "Wait. You're related?"

"A little slow, this one," Khalil teased, as Christian gave him the side eye.

Khalil ignored the outstretched hand and spread his arms. Chaz embraced him, then Vikkas and Jai followed suit. They too, were variations of their father, except Jai had a shock of silver hair at the widow's peak. "We will figure out how we are connected later, but for now, let us find a way to bring your beloved home."

"Chaz and Shaz," Daron said, chuckling. "That's a little close. Might have to call you Shastra instead."

"Not if you want to keep your teeth," Shaz said with a narrow gaze on the tech guru of the group.

"Oooooh," Jai chided with a playful shudder of his shoulders. "A little touchy, are we?"

"So, you're twins," Chaz asked, shooting a gaze between Jai and Vikkas.

"Slow for sure, this one," Vikkas said to his brother, and they all shared a laugh.

Soneni served them gourmet sandwiches, salads, desserts, and beverages as they filtered through all the paperwork Chaz managed to gather since Mandy had been taken away over a week ago. He'd been back and forth to Mississippi securing a local lawyer, trying to get answers, and he was no further along than when he first started.

Christian had already phoned the Kings that first day, who connected them with a judge in Chicago to help get a handle on things until they could arrive. With a sudden infiltration of enemies trying to make their way into Durabia, the Middle Eastern metropolis where the Kings now resided, they had to deal with a national security threat first, then travel to America.

"Well, this is new," Daron said, as he pulled up a schematic of the prison where Mandy now resided. "We've never done a jailbreak."

"And we are not doing one now," Khalil warned, lowering the lid of the laptop so Daron stopped typing. "There is always a weak area when deep-rooted corruption exists. We simply have to find it."

"And exploit it," Vikkas said with a glance at Dro, who had perked up at the mention of a jailbreak.

Shaz leaned forward, resting his chin on his clasped hands. "What do you have in mind?"

"First we uncover their financials," Daron replied, lifting the lid of the keyboard and typing in some information.

"Well, they wouldn't just keep things in a normal way," Jai said over the rim of his glass.

Chaz swept a gaze across everyone. "He has a point."

"We know. Trust us," Daron said, without glancing up from his screen. "We'll have it covered."

"You won't do anything illegal?" Chaz hedged, realizing these men had a dark edge that reminded him of mafia bosses he'd seen in movies.

Vikkas grinned and passed the platter of sandwiches to Shaz who took two off the top. "What's your definition of illegal?"

"That's not funny," Chaz shot back.

"And we are not laughing," Khalil said. "If you expect to obtain the release of your beloved, you cannot presume that it will come under the same process that unfairly put her behind bars."

Chaz shared a speaking glance with Christian, who nodded.

"I know that you're a man of integrity," Jai said, placing his glass on the table. "So are we. What we propose is exposing an already corrupt system."

"That means we have to work outside of their parameters," Shaz offered.

Khalil placed a hand over Chaz's. "And you are going to have to be all right with that."

Chaz grimaced and didn't say anything.

Dro glanced at Chaz as he said, "It's either our way or you—and the triplets—will be visiting Amanda in prison for the rest of her life. They are not letting her go so easy this time. Now that they have her back in their clutches, they want to make an example of her. She killed two officers. They deserved it, but still …"

"All right," Chaz said on a weary sigh. "Whatever brings her home."

"And about that …" Daron pointed to Khalil. "You're up."

Khalil rested his fork on the empty plate. "One more action will make certain that you and your beloved are not impacted by the consequences. We found a way to take back everything that was taken from our family. And more importantly, from me. My name. My wife. My sons. The entire financial holdings of the Maharaj family—American and East Indian." He glanced at Vikkas and Jai. "It is time you, and your family, come home and take your rightful place in Durabia."

Chaz mulled that over for a moment. "I just want to make sure my expectations are in the same place as your reality."

"There's nothing for her here," Jai reminded him. "Her sister, niece, and nephew—the ones who matter to her—are there. Come home."

"I won't live in the palace," Chaz warned, as he thought about how his parents were as good as exiled from Durabia when they secretly fell in love. His mother, a Royal princess, dared to marry someone outside of her parents' arrangement with another kingdom. The family immediately disowned her, leaving the rebellious couple to their fate in government housing in England. His parents put love over royal privilege.

"Fine," Khalil agreed.

"We will need our own space—in the Free Zone."

"Handled," Vikkas said, with a nod that signaled *that's that*.

Khalil stood. "Now let us make that trip to Mississippi and sort out this business with their corrupt court system."

Chapter 22

The loss of Chaz and her children was so profound, Mandy wanted to curl up and die. Unfortunately, she couldn't afford to show weakness in a place like this. They had already nicknamed her The Queen and it wasn't meant as a compliment.

She didn't know about the queen aspect, but she certainly wished her knight in designer suit armor could come in and take her away from this place. Like he had at the airport. Like he had when he appeared on the day the babies were born. Then making sure they—and her—were well situated in a safe and loving environment. Honestly, she hadn't thought about the size of her new family versus the size of her small house. But Chaz had, and took it upon himself to make sure everything she needed was within her reach. Practically spoiling her for any other treatment. He gave her the best, every single day. And she didn't appreciate it for the loving gesture he meant it to be. The flower that was left on her pillow every morning when she awakened. A note from him that started her day. Ones that said *have a splendiferous day* or something like that. She didn't even know splendiferous was a word!

Even the babies had a few of his facial expressions—early on. The gummy smiles. Well, he had all of his teeth, but she recognized him in them all the same. Their eyes, their hair—the texture and dark coloring. Even a few mannerisms, if that was at all possible. He showered them with so much love that she knew her children would not have the same life that she had. Even though she hadn't planned on having children—with him or anyone after the miscarriage and what had caused it—each day with them brought on such joy. Parents who want their children; who would give them the world. Chaz was right. If she ever had the opportunity to be with him again, there would be no room for doubt. Chaz embodied everything a loving mate should have.

Mandy tried to put the angst of missing her babies and Chaz as far back in her mind as she could while going through her day-to-day prison routine. At night, sleep would not come. The lewd suggestions from the women about what they wished to do to her kept her wide awake. She barely managed to have two hours of sleep—if that. Every sound. Every cry. Every moan. The echoes of pain that filtered into her cell. All of them disturbed her soul. She believed that at any time they would pounce and she'd be a victim all over again.

But Mandy, after everything she had been through, was no one's victim. Her sisters Ellena and Melissa had taught her well, and it saved her the night those officers thought she would be easy prey. What she was capable of doing in order to not let that happen again was enough to bring a different kind of fear—that she would spend an eternity in this place.

The lack of sleep finally took its toll and she collapsed on her way to complete another hard day of laundry service.

She woke in the infirmary. Rae was nearby and called for the doctor to come.

"Hey," Dr. Hoyer said. "Back in the land of the living." The woman's face was devoid of any cosmetics. Almost as if she didn't want to call attention to her beauty. Maybe that was a good thing. In this place, beauty could be considered a curse instead of a blessing.

"Do you have any medical history of heart disease?" she asked.

"No."

"High blood pressure?"

"No."

"Diabetes?"

"No."

The doctor jotted the information on a tablet, her brow furrowed with thought. "Have you been … sleeping."

"I—"

"No, she hasn't," Rae supplied, meeting Mandy's warning glare head on. "She's awake all night. Every night. Then tries to get those little cat naps in when she's supposed to be eating. And her milk is not drying up. She's what my mother would have called still stinkin'. She's a new Mom, two, three months on from the looks of her."

"Exhaustion, anxiety, and fever because she can't breastfeed her children," Dr. Hoyer sighed, nodding. "That explains it. How old is the baby?"

"Babies. Triplets. Two months old."

Rae gasped while Dr. Hoyer grimaced and her eyes took on a solemn shadow. "That's truly unfortunate," she said with a weary sigh. "I'm sending you back to the unit to get some rest. And some cream for your breasts should help."

"All right." Mandy's voice broke because she realized the hope she held out that this was all a cosmic joke and she would return to her life and be able to do something as simple as nurse her babies, was now out of her reach.

"What is it that you're afraid of?" the doctor asked.

Mandy filtered through everything that was important in her world. "Two things. Not seeing my babies and Chaz. Not seeing my niece and nephew; my two sisters. And what it'll take to protect myself," she said with a pointed look at Rae. "Being a victim again. Count that all up and I guess that's nine … things."

Dr. Hoyer nodded. "At this rate, you're going to check out of here before there's anything to fear. You need to rest."

"I'll handle it," Rae said, and Mandy didn't quite know what she meant. But she wouldn't ask either. This place had its own set of rules and secrets.

They made the long journey back from the infirmary to their cell block, walking in complete silence. Mandy swayed on her feet although Rae was moving at a measured pace. The fear was crippling. Mandy was afraid that if she let her guard down, they would hurt her, and then she would … No that wouldn't happen. Not again.

She crawled into the bed and lay on her side. Sleep danced and taunted the corners of her consciousness. She still could not give in.

"Go on to sleep, Mandy," Rae commanded, causing Mandy to glance over her shoulder. "I'll make sure you'll be all right."

"So, we're doing promises now?" Nikki asked, her tone hard with displeasure.

She was always vying for Rae's attention right along with Linda and Sabrina.

"No, none of you are going to fuck with her," Rae warned. "Take your asses back over to your side and mind your business."

"You're protecting her?" Sabrina said, leaving her bunk so that she was standing between the other two women. "Why does she—"

"Because I said so, that's why," Rae snapped and everyone in the unit paused and looked their way. Mandy closed her eyes and sighed with relief.

"What makes her so special?" Sabrina demanded, pushing past Linda to stand toe to toe with Rae.

"Depriving herself of sleep is better than what she could do to us."

Nikki scoffed, and Mandy half-opened her eyes in time to see the blonde giving her a disdainful onceover. "And why should we be scared of that?'

"Because I recognize that kind of fear," Rae confessed and her gaze swept across everyone under the sound of her voice. "She's not afraid of what we will do to her, she's afraid of what she'll do to us."

That statement shut everyone down. The entire place became eerily silent.

Rae paced in front of the bed, her face a mask of concern as she said, "The day I put that knife in my husband, I looked in the mirror and saw the same fear in my own eyes that I see in hers. I'd had enough. It took a long ass time—years of beatings, bruises, hospital visits, lost jobs, isolated from my family before it got to that point." She glanced in Mandy's direction. "Sabrina had someone working in records and told me why the guards have such a hard-on for Mandy. This woman killed two prison guards who tried to rape her. Shot one, killed the other with her bare hands, and blinded the last one. Picture that, one woman took out three men because she didn't want them to rape her. Imagine what she would do to one of us."

Heads and gazes whipped toward Mandy as shocked and doubtful expressions gave away how they felt about that admission.

"Yeah, I could do something— give her to me," a voice taunted through the bars on the door. "Bet I can get a few feels and rocks off. Bet I can make her sit roll over … beg and crawl. Hand her here. Saw the breast milk leaking through. Come here honey I got cookies."

"Sorry, we don't speak beast." Rae walked over to the bars and stared the woman down. "Go back to your corner of Hell. Let one of them rats eat you raw."

The woman at the bars stuck her hand through the steel and Rae sidestepped her with ease.

"You really want that arm broken, don't you? I can do it for you. Reach in here again. Happy to do it." She chuckled as the woman and her little entourage walked away.

Rae sauntered toward the center of the unit and spoke to the rest of the women who had watched the exchange. "She's like us. Might be a little prim and proper, but more like us than we want to believe. We all reached that point where we're not going to allow anyone else to take something we're not willing to give."

Rae included all of them in her gaze. Sounds from the other units had ceased as well. Everyone must have been listening in.

"She is past that point. Killing one of us means that she will never go home. *That's* what she's afraid of. She's got a life out there. She's got three newborn babies out there. She's got love out there. Mandy simply wants to do her time and go home. And we're going to let her." Rae stepped forward until she was nearly nose to nose with Nikki. "Anyone who fucks with her after I've said don't, will have to answer to me."

Nikki inched back, lowered her gaze to the concrete.

"You know she don't belong here," Rae said. "The system down here got her on some dumb shit. Same as a whole lot of us. If she can't be safe nowhere else, she's gonna be safe with us.

Only then did Mandy allow sleep to claim her.

Chapter 23

Chaz ended his call and hurried toward the foyer the moment Karen informed him that Susan Keller was there to see him.

Every ounce of anger came to the forefront and he wondered why the hell she would want to show up unannounced. Chaz had already been under an enormous amount of stress working, making the flights to Mississippi to put things in order, and taking care of the kids while Mandy was in prison. The thought of seeing his ex-wife's face made him so furious, his face flushed with heat. She had his woman taken, away from him, away from their children. That was the lowest of low.

Thankfully, the Kings of the Castle were working some kind of magic, and that meant Chaz had only a week to gather his entire life, his children, and his house staff, and prepare to make moves the moment they said it was time to leave. Christian put a lot of stock in these men, and the fact that a few of them were part of his bloodline gave him a sense of peace. He'd looked into the organization—The Castle—and liked what they stood for.

"Why are you here?" he asked as he stalked into the living room.

Susan inched away, taken aback by his tone. Then she squared her shoulders and regrouped. "I came to see how you're doing," she said, stepping forward. "See if you needed any ... help."

He threw up a hand to stop her from coming too close.

"We both seem to be suffering behind all of this," she continued.

"You mean behind the mess you created," he said, chest heaving in an effort to contain his pissosity. If that was even a word.

"It's not my fault that she didn't have proper permission to travel to Jamaica," Susan said with a haughty lift of her chin, that superior attitude firmly on display.

"Not your fault," he spat. "It's *never* your fault, is it? Why. Are. You. Here?"

Susan peered around him and was met with the glaring faces of Soneni, Karen, and Nita, who were on standby in case they needed to cart Susan out of the house.

"I thought we could talk." She lowered her voice. "Put some of the enmity between us to rest."

"Really? After you conspired to put my beloved in prison, merely out of spite," he roared. "We were completely over and yet you still found a way to make my life miserable."

"I didn't mean —"

"I didn't listen to Rayna," he said, adjusting his stance so that he leaned against the wall next to the door. "She told me early on that your whole purpose was to get next to me. I thought she was simply jealous. A trait I despise because we are supposed to be spiritually enlightened enough to realize that what is for us, is something no one can take away."

He shook his head, thinking of the woman who introduced him to Susan to her own detriment. "I didn't see it then, but I recognize it now. You schemed and did everything you could to come between me and Rayna until she saw no further benefit in dealing with your machinations, as well as my unwillingness to see you for the conniving, manipulative woman you are. I hurt that woman unnecessarily, and I will forever carry that burden."

"She wasn't good enough for you," Susan snarled, slamming a hand to his chest, causing Soneni and Karen to move in closer.

"And who are you to determine that?" he spat, holding up a hand to halt their movements. "Just who the hell are you?"

Susan reached for him. "She couldn't move you forward into being an international star."

"Do you think I cared about any of that?" he said, shaking off her touch. "I wanted a wife, some children, to travel the world—yes. But simple pleasures satisfy me."

"You are royalty and you are so talented," she protested. "It was sacrilege for you to be so small."

"And it was up to you to do that? Up to you—to make it your life's mission to bring the poor, small- time East Indian-Durabian man into the world spotlight? All by yourself, right?" He sighed in disgust. "Your elitism and what is it they're calling it these days?—Privilege—is showing, Susan. Every ounce of it."

Color flushed her face. "You were only with her out of obligation."

"And I was with you all those years of lying, stringing me along, out of … what?"

"It's not the same thing," she said, waving him off.

"Oh, but it is." He chuckled. "I'm done with this conversation. Please make use of the exit and do not return to her home—"

"Your home," Susan corrected, screeching at the top of her voice. "She didn't have a dime, just like you didn't."

"Hers," he insisted. "Just like I am. Hers. Her house. Her children. Her beloved." Chaz gave Susan a megawatt smile. "Not sure what you thought coming here would accomplish, but I forgive you. If that's what you need to hear. I definitely forgive you, and that's for my own sanity. But I need to make this loud and crystal clear." He narrowed his gaze on her. "Stay as far away from me as fucking possible."

"I never meant to—"

"But you did," he snapped. "And we—these little ones and myself—are paying the price for your evil, your jealousy, your need to control and manipulate. For someone who was supposed to be so spiritual, you took a fast slide into darkness." He gritted his teeth, then asked, "Did you think about how this would affect my children? To lose their mother before they even realized who she was?" He opened the front door wider. "Stay away from us. Keep your toxicity in California or Mississippi where it belongs."

Chapter 24

Mandy awakened to find the women situated on the floor around her bed, playing cards. She shifted, and all of them tensed.

"Hey, sleeping beauty," Rae teased

Those words brought Chaz to mind, and her heart constricted. She had wasted so much time and all he wanted to do was love her.

"We thought we were going to have to find Prince Charming to wake you up."

"Tough time on that one," Sabrina said dryly, slapping a card onto the makeshift table. "All the guards are frogs—even the women."

Laughter abounded. Even Mandy had to chuckle at that one.

"How long have I been out?" She felt like cotton resided in her mouth and her belly was so empty, her stomach was kissing her back.

"Sixteen hours."

She blinked several times to clear her vision. "Wait, what?"

"Yep," Linda said, tossing out an ace of clubs on top of the other cards. "We've had breakfast, lunch, dinner, and breakfast again. They let us bring you a little something because chow ain't up again until lunch."

"Thank you," she said, accepting the breakfast wrap and water from Sabrina. "What are you playing?"

"Bid Whist," Rae answered.

Mandy took a sip of water and let it swirl around her mouth. "Bid? With no kitty?" All heads turned her way, and she shrugged. "Without the kitty, it's just like Spades. The kitty changes the game. I'm just saying."

Rae roared with laughter. "Well, come on down and show us what you're working with, Miss Mandy."

"All right." She tried to get down off the bunk but her legs wouldn't cooperate.

"You need to stretch a little." Sabrina and Linda rushed to help lower her from the bed.

"I need to do a little yoga to get myself back together."

"You do yoga," Rae asked, her shock evident. "I thought that was a white folks thing."

"That's where you're wrong. Yoga is for everyone."

He had given her a gift in teaching her about intentions, mantras, and yoga. She was fully prepared to share that gift with the other women. Chaz had, for all intents and purposes, stepped up in her life as the man who wanted, needed, desired, and loved her—and he showed that first in getting her to accept herself using yoga and all those other methods. What more could a woman ask for?

She tried to stretch but it was cut short when her kidneys made their presence known. "I'm going to need a trip to the potty first."

"We'll get you there," the petite Asian said. "But after that you're on your own, girlfriend."

"And maybe a shower, too?"

Sabrina gave her a thumbs up. "We got you."

"Thank you."

She showered, dressed, and all the while her unit mates stood guard. Some of the others gave them curious stares on the way back to their cell.

"So, The Queen has guards now?" Sharla, a buxom Amazon, sauntered up to Nikki. "Must be some mighty good snatch—"

"Hey, it's not like that," Sabrina said. "She just came back from med, that's all."

"So that mean she's ready for—"

Three of Mandy's cell mates blocked her path. "No."

The woman stood with both hands on her hips. "Who the hell are you to—"

"They said no," Rae roared and all eyes turned to her. "No one lays a hand on her."

Sharla's smile was slow in coming. "She's your property? Even with the kinda heat attached to her ass? Make it easy on yourself, Just hand her over."

"She's with us," Rae confirmed. "That's all you need to know."

"You can't watch her all the time," Sharla warned, giving a smile that didn't quite reach her eyes. "Eye for an eye, Queen." She executed a perfect curtsy before she turned away.

"Right, but the moment you decide to test me, is the day you decide to die."

That threat hung in the air for a moment before grumbles of dissent followed.

"It's like that, huh?"

Rae tilted her head. "And it's not me you need to be afraid of."

"Is that right?" The woman's tone was sarcastic.

"She killed a man. Actually, two of them. They tried to take something she wasn't willing to give 'em. And those were men who were twice her strength."

"If she's so tough, why was she acting all scared—"

"She wasn't scared of us," Rae countered, poking a finger in the bigger woman's chest. "She's scared of having to do it again. Listen to that one more time. You know that type of fear. It's what landed most of us here in the first place. So, take a chance if you want to, and if she doesn't kill you … I will." Rae leaned in. "Mandy McCoy is off limits—period."

Chapter 25

Chaz sat on a wooden bench between Vikkas and Dro for the emergency hearing. Daron had positioned himself in front of Shaz. Patricia Breedlaw, one of the judges from Chicago they had consulted, had also taken the time out of her all-too-busy schedule to make the trip to Mississippi. The purpose of her presence was to observe how many points of reference they could use for the mishandling of Mandy's case to be taken further up the judicial chain. If they meant to stay under the radar, the striking strawberry-blonde hair and honey complexion, would not accomplish that in any form.

A reporter from the *Sun Herald* was also nearby. She was now steady on the radar, thanks to Dro.

The deputy brought Mandy out, guiding her past the people sitting in the courtroom. Her knees nearly buckled at the sight of Chaz, who stood the moment he laid eyes on her. The deputy helped Mandy regain her balance as Daron yanked Chaz back down before he caught the attention of the judge.

Too late.

Judge Stewart looked down the bridge of his nose, peering at them with dull, lifeless blue eyes. The men made a formidable sight. All in black suits and poker faces.

"Why are all these additional people here?" he asked with a pointed look at his bailiff, then to the Kings and Chaz.

No one answered.

"This is a routine case," he continued.

Still the Kings and Chaz said nothing.

"Not so routine," Mandy's currently ineffective counsel said. "Since she's hiring new private counsel and plans to reopen the case against her."

"Isn't this a matter of a," the judge paused, scanning the contents of the folder. "Parole violation."

"It's not that simple," Shaz said, getting to his feet. "Case transcripts show a number of discrepancies in how Ms. McCoy's case was handled and what was applicable by law."

Vikkas stood next to Shaz and added, "She had a right to private counsel, but you denied her the opportunity and proceeded with the public defender instead. That's just one of several points we're aiming to follow up on here."

The judge's eyes narrowed to slits. He fingered the edges of the document he held, then dropped them to point to the rows where Chaz and the Kings were situated. "My chambers. Now."

They all stood. Ready to do battle.

"Get these others out of here, too," he said, waving his hand in a dismissive motion.

***

As the barrel-chested bailiff turned the reporter away, then escorted everyone to the judge's luxuriously decorated chambers, Mandy asked, "Where are my babies?"

Chaz leaned in and whispered, "They're already on the plane with Soneni, Karen, and Nita."

"Plane?" she asked, clearly mystified.

"Later," he murmured.

"How are they?" she asked, in a tearful voice.

Chaz pressed a kiss to her temple. "Missing you. Just like me, baby. Just. Like. Me."

"Who are these people?" she asked with a sweeping glance at the group of men she didn't know.

"Christian brought in help. Lots of it."

Mandy relaxed and smiled. "I love that boy."

"Better not let him hear you call him that," Chaz warned and she chuckled.

Somehow, she felt a sliver of hope. Being this close to Chaz was something that she focused on during her daily meditations with Rae and the other women every day. Every morning, together, they prayed for peace, doing the mantras that Chaz had taught her. They did the forgiveness work that had been effective for so many people. First it was her immediate "crew", then others joined in.

Later she added the Intender's Circle methods, where each woman wrote and then spoke their intentions and outcomes for their lives. She then added yoga and meditation and it seemed the entire vibration of the place changed. Work became easier, and fewer fights and arguments erupted on the block. There wasn't much they could do about where they were situated, but they could do things to change how they felt inside, and for each other.

In the wood-paneled room, Judge Breedlaw laid out the scenario, citing everything Judge Stewart had done wrong, completely disregarding Mississippi law in dealing with Mandy's case. Then she stated the way things were going to be for him to rectify the situation—immediately.

The district attorney parted his mouth to speak, but Judge Stewart held up a hand to ward him off.

When Chaz heard the facts put the way Judge Breedlaw outlined them, he was furious. Mandy had a raw deal early in life, from her family, then in marriage, then with this man. No wonder she had trust issues. She had been catching it from all sides since day one and the judge, the deputies, and this district attorney had done major damage in an effort to feed their greed.

"What you can't afford is too much publicity," Daron reminded Judge Stewart. "Your little debtor's prison scheme is America's worst kept secret—they let you run with whatever."

"There is no way you're going to come up in here, in my house, and tell me how to run things," the judge said through his teeth.

Shaz leaned in so he was mere inches from the judge. "I will call every attorney in our arsenal to come down, suit up, take on every case you ever laid eyes on, then flood the area with so much money, they will have you spinning your wheels."

"Then, we will put our money behind whoever we can," Khalil said, crossing one leg over the other. "And we will unseat you for another judge that actually will uphold the law and not use it to line their own pockets."

"And that's just for shits and giggles," Jai added.

While the exchange between the district attorney, Judges Breedlaw and Stewart, along with Vikkas and Shaz continued, Mandy huddled with Chaz.

"And I can't leave my girls in there like that," she said, causing all eyes to focus her way. "They protected me, once they came to know me, and they kept anyone else from hurting me."

"What are their names?" Dro asked, leaning back as she rattled off their details like they were phone numbers.

"You remember their inmate numbers like that?"

"That's what they called us by most times," she answered, placing her hand in Chaz's. "Hard to forget."

Dro typed in something on his tablet, then passed it to Daron.

"So, now you're just trying to break everyone free?" Judge Stewart squawked, glowering at her. "I don't care what they have on your case, but I can't allow that."

Shaz nodded to Vikkas, who angled his body so he could check Daron's screen as he spoke. "Every single one of these women have a right to file a civil suit against you, the State of Mississippi, and everyone in on the scheme. They don't have to win, but it will force the right people to comb through … certain documents and people's finances, as well as contracts with businesses in the area that are kicking you back with money under the table. Then the world will know just how deep your corruption goes."

"Watch how fast those people connected with this distance themselves from you," Shaz added.

The judge smiled. "Eye for an eye. Can't outrun the long arm of the law. I could always—"

"Hide the documents before anyone can scrutinize them," Daron supplied, chuckling. "You could try, but nothing is ever truly hidden in the cyberworld."

"And while we're sitting here laying things out," Vikkas said. "You won't believe how easy it is to *duplicate* those records and put the digital ones somewhere else for safe-keeping."

"There is always an electronic imprint," Khalil said with a nod.

Vikkas sighed and perched on the arm of the nearest chair. "Not to mention, people who don't want to go down with the ship might be willing to do anything to cover their own asses."

"You know," Dro added. "Like making sure the most important documents don't get shredded and are passed to people who are paying more than you." He winked. "You know, that sort of thing."

The silence that came after those words was profound.

"You city boys aren't so smart after all," Judge Stewart taunted to break the tense moment. "Why would you tell me your game plan unless—"

Khalil moved forward, smiling as he said, "Smart is relative. Intelligence is Divine. As you were saying …"

Sounding strangled, Judge Stewart asked, "Wh-what do you want?"

"So, we're adding that we want immediate release of all of these women—" He slid the names and information across the desk.

"And a formal review of every case you've handled since you've been on the bench, to issue a more appropriate lawful sentence or time served for the ones who have been in long enough." Judge Breedlaw was so angry, a vein throbbed at her temple. "And that goes for Judges Dawley, Steyer, and Bloomberg."

"I don't control them, any more than Susan's father…." he said with a dismissive wave.

"Yes, about that. So, you know Susan, Chaz's ex-wife. Interesting. We discovered that, too. And all the other rich daddies with a proclivity for vulnerable women. You can get through to them." Khalil nodded once. "The warden, too. And we mean *right now*. You can easily issue an order vacating the conviction of Amanda Renee McCoy, and also a finding of factual innocence and order that she be released immediately."

All the Kings whipped their focus in Khalil's direction. He smiled when Judge Breedlaw did the same. Khalil shrugged and said, "Research," and winked.

Dro settled in the seat where Vikkas was perched on the armrest, then crossed one leg over the other, watching as Judge Stewart's blank stare signaled he was still processing all of this bad news and trying to come out ahead.

"You know, that secret Friday night poker game where you have ... select female inmates removed to serve your needs and those of Dawley, Steyer, and Bloomberg ..."

Judge Stewart's eyes widened in shock, then fear at hearing Khalil's words.

"Was that part of the rehabilitation program or was it something—you know—*different*," Judge Breedlaw said, and her dark-brown eyes flashed with fire. "Inquiring minds and all that. Just thought I'd mention that the last ones were recorded. Amazing how much the inmates you've wronged have to tell us about what you've been doing."

The judge's skin paled as he laid both hands on top of the desk, they were trembling in an effort to contain his rage. "You were supposed to stay put. You were supposed to stay in your place," he snarled at Mandy. "And you went on a little pleasure trip. Didn't you? Despite them forcing me to let you serve your time in Chicago, you still defied me! You defied this court."

Everyone in the room remained silent after that outburst. Seconds ticked by as everything fell into place.

"Now I don't have to wonder why those guards felt they could do what they did to me. They took their cues from you," Mandy choked out. "And I want my money back. Every damn dime. You want those rapists and their families to be taken care of or *made whole* as you said, then you pay them. And that voice on the phone—"

"That big blonde bitch," he breathed.

"Sharla, her name is Sharla," Mandy shot back. "Funny how her

American accent faded when she talked to her children. What was the price for her?"

Chaz looked at Mandy, then the judge who growled, "A lot less than it was for you."

"Shame that they killed the wrong woman in Jamaica," Mandy said causing Chaz to tighten his hold on her hand. "That bullet was meant for me. Wasn't it?"

"Well, someone had to keep you quiet," the judge countered. "Since you didn't know what else to do with that mouth, after I asked you to."

"You depraved bastard," Chaz said through his teeth.

Mandy almost had to put her body between the judge and Chaz as she let out a dismal laugh. "That man, the deputy, right?" she said peering at him. "The one who was following me. The only one who had just as much to lose as you do."

"What are you talking about," Vikkas asked, scanning her face and the other kings also narrowed their gazes in her direction.

"The only one of the three who lived," Chaz said, nodding as realization kicked in. "Lost a body part in the process. An eye for an eye, right?"

Mandy kept her focus on the judge who had lost even more of his coloring. "So, he missed raping and then killing me in Jamaica. Then you had your cronies plant enough seeds of doubt to make me doubt myself and everything I hold dear."

She held up a hand the moment he opened his mouth to speak. "Don't bother lying. Sharla told me everything over yoga and mantras. She told me the whole sordid story—even you having someone bring in burner phones for her to make those calls."

Mandy shook her fist at him. "You threatened to take her kids. Her *kids*, you sick bastard! And you used her husband to make the rest of those calls, knowing the man is dying from lung cancer." She stood and

Chaz moved along with her to put an arm around her shoulders.

"Every damn dime. Every single dime you stole from me," she said, wagging a finger in the judge's face. "I want it back for me, for Sharla, and for all of them!"

"What she said," Chaz chimed in, holding her trembling form. "Every damn dime."

"But that's nearly a—"

"You have it," Daron said, turning his tablet's screen to the judge. "Stashed in the Cayman Islands and Swiss accounts. You have it. So, play broke if you want to. We'll shake those skeletons in your closet so hard, you'll think they've been living in seven-below weather all this time."

"Let's ride," Shaz said, as he stood. "We have places to be."

Khalil tapped Judge Stewart's desk. "Write the order for her release, and the others, and another one to expunge their records immediately."

"What does that matter?" Vikkas said under his breath. "She won't be here."

"It matters to her," Khalil said with a glance in Mandy and Chaz's direction. "And Amanda McCoy is not going to see the inside of that prison again. She is staying with us."

"That's not possible." The judge practically growled causing the district attorney to flinch. "She has to be processed out."

"She shouldn't have been in there in the first place," Chaz said with a pointed glare at the judge. "And you, the district attorney, and the warden were also in on this. Make it happen."

Chapter 26

Mandy stood with her face turned up to the sun. She pulled in a deep breath and let it out, scarcely daring to believe she'd be home soon. This morning, the four women who were the closest to her—Rae, Linda, Nikki, and Sabrina—sat with her on the floor of their cell to speak an intention for the best possible experience today. They aligned with her for the most beneficent outcome, for the highest and best good for herself and *everyone* involved.

When they were done, she took out a sheet of paper and wrote the names of the men who had harmed her, including her ex, the judge, the lawyers, her grandfather, her uncle, then tossed her mother's and Dorsey's name in too. She released as much of the guilt and anger as she could.

Then she took things a step further and wrote the words she remembered from Chaz's journal—each letter, each syllable, each nuance, and all of it gave her a feeling of hope and elation. No matter what the outcome, she had him to hold onto.

The prison walls behind them caused a shiver of alarm to whip through her.

"Are you all right, my love?" Chaz asked, with one arm around her.

"As long as things continue the way they have today and I get to see my babies ..."

"Don't worry." Chaz touched his lips to hers. "Everything will be fine." Then he held his hand out to Jai who placed that purple velvet bag in his hands. Chaz pulled out the journal and flipped to the last page before pressing Mandy's hand to the new inscription that read ... *our story continues* ...

The Kings parked their vehicles and gathered around Khalil for a few minutes. So far, they had all the documents they needed. Mandy was grateful she was able to remain with them. Inside the prison walls, the warden was rushing through the processing to release her and the other women from the prison.

"We're not going to let him get away with any of that, right?" Shaz asked.

"Hell no," Judge Breedlaw replied. "The justice department is on their way to scoop up him and his cronies."

"So, you lied to him," Mandy mused, eyes widening with understanding.

"We didn't lie," Vikkas answered with a grin. "We just didn't tell the truth, the whole truth, and nothing but the truth."

Chaz chuckled as the men nodded with knowing expressions. "I like the way you think."

Khalil then went on to explain the game plan of moving her, the triplets, and their staff to Durabia to let the dust settle.

"Do you think my friends can come with us?" she asked.

"Lady, you want a whole lot of sugar for a dime," Daron chided, frowning.

Mandy averted her gaze. "It will be a fresh start for all of us."

"But they have family here," Vikkas warned, narrowing a gaze on her. "They might not even want to go."

"What will it cost? What can I do?" Mandy asked. "They won't ever have normal lives even after this dies down."

"Here's what we'll do," Shaz said, tapping his chin with one finger. "We have a short window of time. Let's get them out first, since we have that option."

Mandy gave a grateful nod. "Let's do that before Judge Breedlaw's people make it down and one of them undoes what you've just done by putting everyone back in to sort things out."

"She has a point," Vikkas said.

Daron passed a specialized tablet to Dro. "All right let's see what we can get done."

* * *

An officer yelled a series of inmate numbers and the patter of booted feet echoed down the corridor. "Gather your things," Officer Walker called out. "You're being released today."

The numbers he specified belonged to Rae, Linda, Nikki, and Sabrina.

Nikki slid off the top bunk. "What?"

"Is this some kind of joke?" Sabrina asked, putting the cards aside and getting to her feet.

Linda's head whipped to Rae who was sitting in a basic yoga pose. "Are we being pranked?"

The other three women stood with their mouths open.

"You've got fifteen minutes to pack your stuff," the second officer said. "Move."

The women froze.

Sabrina and Nikki shared a glance. "No, something's up."

"I have twelve years left on my sentence." Rae shook her head. "Naw, y'all just taking us somewhere to kill us like you're doing over there in the men's prison. Sixteen dead." The others around her nodded. That news had put fear in everyone. Those mysterious deaths signaled that something deeper and darker was going on. "Y'all just taking them out like animals. And that's the ones we know about 'cause they have families that made some noise and it's on the tube."

"Fourteen minutes," Officer Walker said, glaring at Rae who met her look head on, still wanting answers.

Sabrina went past Linda and rushed to the window. "Hey. Hey. Everybody, come look at this."

All the women in the unit ran to the windows in the cells to look at the yard below.

"Isn't that …?"

"Yeah, it is."

"Mandy still in uniform, but not in cuffs," Rae said.

"But what if it's a trick?" Linda asked, looking to Rae for reassurance that she couldn't provide. "You know, some kind of thing to make us think it's legit."

"Listen up," Officer Walker said, "You didn't hear it from me, but one of the courthouse clerks said McCoy's got a team of high-powered lawyers and journalists to look into everyone's case."

Sharla moved from the window to grip the steel bars. "Even mine?"

Officer Walker nodded. "Even yours."

"That's what's up," Rae said with a wide grin. It hadn't escaped her notice that the five women who diligently affirmed their intentions, their forgiveness work, and meditated everyday, were the ones that were leaving today.

"Looks like all that praying finally paid off," Nikki said.

"Doesn't mean that all of y'all are walking out, but—"

"Means, you'll be out of a job," Sabrina taunted. "If they look real close at what those crooks did to everyone."

"Never." Walker laughed, gesturing to the rest of the women behind them. "There's enough folks committing crimes to keep us in business until my great, great, grandchildren grow old."

"The sad thing is, that isn't wrong," Rae said, shaking her head.

"Judge picked the wrong one this time. She's got people—people bigger than him and now she's got 'em on the ropes," Nikki quipped, punching the air as though fighting an imaginary opponent.

"Mandy is standing on the other side of the gate with all those men for a reason." Rae turned to face everyone. "She trusted us. Her crew. Now we have to trust her. Let's move."

"I just wonder why it's so sudden," Linda said, gathering her things from the shelves.

"I don't know, and I don't care," Sabrina shot back. "Let's haul some ass."

Within ten minutes they had their belongings crammed into sheets and boxes, and gave away the rest to the women who were left behind.

"What about Mandy's stuff?"

"Let's take it with us," Rae said. "If she was coming back inside, she'd already be here."

"Is this for real?" Sabrina said, trying to hide her excitement.

Walker handed each of them a set of documents.

Nikki chuckled. "Who knew that protecting The Queen would land us on home court?"

The guard guided them through the maze, toward freedom. "Y'all just got lucky."

"No, we've been blessed," Rae said, trailing her to the doors.

Chapter 27

The four of them stepped out of the building, blinded by the sunlight and warmed by the Mississippi heat. Only a moment went by before they zeroed in on Mandy. She gripped the fence, but her expression was dead serious. Not the smile one would expect when seeing newly-sprung friends. She glanced over her shoulder to the SUV limos parked in a line, evidently waiting on them, then back to Rae.

Rae, who had visions of Shadow Bay, the east coast town she called home, dancing in her mind, instantly picked up that something was wrong. "Come on y'all, let's hit it. With a quickness."

She didn't have to tell them twice. They quickened the pace and swept those last few yards to freedom.

"You'll be back," one of the guards taunted, placing his hands on his waist as he stood aside and let them out.

"Not if I can help it—" Nikki retorted.

"That's my point," he said, laughing along with the other men.

They embraced Mandy, tightly.

"Ladies, I'd love to extend this reunion," Mandy said. "But I have good news and bad news."

"Okay," Rae said, peering at her as the other women inched back to give her room. "What's the bad news?"

"Right now, you have two choices," she answered. "Come with me to Durabia, the place Chaz is from originally, or take your chances by going to your families."

"So why is that bad news?" Linda asked.

"What do you mean take our chances." Rae's gaze narrowed on Mandy. "What did you do?"

"Kind of …" she shrugged. "Strong-armed a judge into securing your release." She then gave them the Cliff Notes version of what happened in chambers a few hours before.

Rae gave her a power bump—fists touching each other. "Gangster," she said, grinning.

"No doubt, but what also has happened is that a legal oversight committee and the Department of Justice will be brought in to review all of the cases tried before Judges Dawley, Steyer, and Bloomberg."

"And that committee might unravel what you just did," Rae said.

"We're not sure which way it'll go," Mandy said.

Frowning, Linda asked, "So, the choice is …"

"Get into the limos over there and they'll take us directly to the airport and to my new home in the Middle East."

"Time is of the essence," Dro said to Chaz at a pitch loud enough for Mandy and the women to hear.

Sabrina clutched her bag to her chest. "I won't get to say goodbye to my family?"

Mandy looked over her shoulder at Chaz, who circled an index finger to signal they needed to speed things up. She focused on the group of women and shook her head.

"But I haven't seen them in years," Linda protested with a panicked expression that mirrored Nikki's.

"If we were still locked up, you weren't gonna get to see 'em anyway," Rae said. "So what's the difference?"

"Well, we …"

Chaz marched over to the group and put his hands on Mandy's shoulders. "Beloved, we don't have time to convince anyone of any damn thing. You wanted them out, we,"—He gestured to the handsome, formidable men standing near the SUVs —"made that happen. You wanted them safe with you. They have the choice." He inhaled, obviously trying to remain calm. "But we can't stand around while they figure it out. I promised to keep you safe and if I have to throw you over my shoulder and put you into the car my damn self to get you to the plane, I will. These few weeks without you have been torture. You are not going to deprive me of Heaven just because they wish to remain in Hell."

"Well damn," Rae said, grinning. "Boss man!"

"Ladies, it's been nice," Mandy said, pivoting and moving in the direction that meant freedom and being with her man. "But Aretha said it best in Dr. Feelgood. So, I have to go."

Chaz was right behind her.

"But what about jobs?" Rae asked, inching forward. "How will we make a living—"

"That's all going to be worked out," Daron said, tapping his watch.

Rae's feet aimed in the direction that would help her catch up to her new friends who were fast putting distance between the prison and their past. "Cool. I'm rolling with you."

"Me too," Linda said with a two-step.

Nikki nodded, breaking into sprint. "Me three."

Sabrina first moved forward, then froze and hung back. "I want to see my children and my husband."

"Understandable." Chaz gestured to the last car behind them. "Your ride's that way. Good luck."

Mandy crossed the distance and embraced Sabrina. "Take care of yourself."

Sabrina sighed. "Y'all can't just let us—"

"No," Mandy answered as Chaz caught back up with her and tugged at the jumpsuit. "Unfortunately."

"I want my woman out of this place. Period." Chaz leveled a hard gaze on Sabrina. "If you're still able to make it later, that's fine. But for now. I'm not taking any chances. We are getting the hell out of Dodge."

Chapter 28

Mandy glanced out of the rear window as the vehicle carrying Sabrina in the opposite direction disappeared. There were now four SUVs speeding toward the airport. "We couldn't allow just an hour or two for them to ...?"

"Love, we'll work everything out when we get there." Chaz cradled her in his arms. "But we can't arrange a damn thing if you're in the belly of the beast. Wait with them and you would pay the cost. Our children would pay that cost. I would pay that cost. And I'm done paying. I want my woman."

She settled into his arms. "Point taken."

"Not to be cold, but possession is nine-tenths of the law," he whispered, pressing a kiss to her cheek. "You're in my possession now. And I have no intention of letting them take you from me again."

"Now that's some sexy shit right there," Rae said with an appreciative nod.

"So, he's the Yoga dude?" Linda asked, giving him a onceover. "Who taught you all that stuff you taught us?"

"Yes, among other things."

Mandy gripped the security bar as the vehicle lurched forward, certain she heard sirens. "Why are they driving so fast?"

"Because the clerk called Daron," Vikkas answered. "He gave him a tip that the Department of Justice is gunning to round up everyone Judge Stewart released to send them back through the proper channels."

"So, Sabrina's going back to jail?" Linda asked as her shoulders slumped.

Vikkas nodded. "Afraid so."

"Call Grayson Daniels," Dro said to Daron. "Have him take her to Chicago, instead."

Khalil gestured toward Jai. "Send another car for her children, take them there right after we make sure she's secured in the Castle."

"What are you doing?" Mandy said, gripping Jai's shoulder.

"Sabrina sacrificed her freedom. We can at least make sure she sees her children before going back in," he answered.

"They won't be looking at airports right away," Dro said, "We submitted paperwork saying that we were taking them—" he gestured to Rae and the other women—"to whatever address they had on file."

"Before they figure it out," Shaz glanced back at them. "We'll be wheels up."

"Heads up," Dro said snatching his eyes from the screen and putting his focus on Chaz, Mandy, and the other women. He passed the tablet to Daron. "The second we hit that tarmac in the private wing you all hightail it to the plane. You hear me?"

"Don't stop until you're up those stairs and on the aircraft," Daron commanded, scanning the information for himself. "Once we're in the air, we're under a different level of protection."

The sirens in the distance seemed to be closing in on them.

"I swear I want to laugh so hard," Rae said. "The Queen's men. A real-life jail break. Go figure."

"We can do this." Mandy smiled with confidence she didn't feel.

"I'm afraid," Rae confessed. "You know that, right?"

"Trust me. I am too." Mandy touched Chaz's chest. "But I love this man with my whole heart. And if he's made a way for us to get gone, I'm following his lead."

"Here," he said, handing her a document.

"This says I'm already your wife." She passed one finger over the photo affixed to the passport.

"For now."

She looked into his eyes. "Is that what you want?"

"Most definitely."

"I would be honored to be your wife," she said. "It's not every day a man breaks a woman out of jail."

"And her friends," Rae said. "Don't forget the friends, too."

Chaz passed the other ladies their papers. "Need you to sign these real quick so Daron can have your Durabia identification processed."

"Passports that say we're Durabian Citizens," Rae said after scanning the sheet. "But you're asking to put these under our maiden names."

"Slows the authorities down if they try to trace you," Shaz piped up.

"Vikkas and Khalil … they look a lot like you." Mandy said as she stared at them. "Who are they, really?"

"Family."

"Wait a minute," she said, peering at the oldest man in the crew. "He's *that* Khalil? Khalil Germaine Maharaj. Related to the ruler of Durabia. The man who's married to my sister. You're that kind of royal?"

Chaz shrugged. "Distant, but yes."

"So, she really is The Queen." Nikki gave a nod of approval.

"Do you know what's going to happen to us in Durabia?" Rae asked, nudging Nikki into silence.

"A lot better than what can happen here," Chaz mused.

"Need to put the pedal to the metal," Khalil said to the driver. "I do not want Daron or Dro to have to put a bullet in someone to get our point across."

"You're the one who's trigger happy," Shaz protested.

"See, why do you wish to bring up old things?" Khalil shot back.

The Kings burst into laughter.

Rae's eyes widened with shock. "Dude is packing?"

"They all are," Chaz said. "Those bulges aren't because they're happy to see your cell mates."

"Woman, what kind of family you got?" Rae asked, adjusting her seatbelt.

Mandy smiled and laid her head against Chaz's chest. "The best kind."

Chapter 29

"The flight was a beast," Rae groaned the moment they alighted from the plane.

"Thirteen hours." Linda stretched and let loose with a yawn that was enough to soak up all the oxygen in the entire area. "Damn."

"Those compression socks have me feeling like a grandma," Nikki said looking down at the tight thigh high material covering her legs.

"I don't know, they're kind of sexy on you," Rae teased with a wink.

All of them laughed at Rae's quip.

The only heartbreaking moment on the trip came when Mandy tried to see if she had enough milk to nurse the babies. She was sorely disappointed. Chaz consoled her as best he could as she sobbed into his chest.

A caravan of SUVs awaited once they passed through customs, security, and made it to the entrance specifically for royals.

"In style, too," Rae leaned in to whisper to Mandy. "Private jet. Limos. He's spoiling us."

Nikki grinned. "It's not like we aren't due for some good treatment."

They had pulled off, but the driver glanced in the rearview mirror and said, "Are these people supposed to be in one of the cars?"

Chaz and Mandy glanced out of the rear window. Christian and Blair raced toward them trying to catch up, waving their hands. Mandy was out of the limo in a heartbeat, before the vehicle came to a complete stop.

"Honey, wait a minute—"

Chaz was talking to himself. He blinked twice and she was already in their arms.

"Are we going to be all right?" Rae asked, eyeing the exchange between Mandy and her family.

He wouldn't tell them that housing was going to be a little tight as Dro and Daron were working out the logistics of securing a place that would keep them close but also allow them to acclimate to their new life in Durabia.

This was not how Chaz planned to start *his* new life in Durabia with three additional guests who had questionable backgrounds, but if this was what it took for Mandy to feel settled, so be it.

All of them were loaded into luxury vehicles and soon arrived at a triplex penthouse in the heart of Durabia.

"We need to buy some time," Daron said, after checking his phone. "Hassan, another Royal, is getting things together to situate the women at the palace."

While Christian and Blair made much of the babies, Mandy's focus shifted to her friends. "Can't they just stay with us?"

"Love," Chaz said in a mild tone. "They prepared a nine-bedroom home to accommodate us, the children, and our staff. It will be too crowded."

"Too crowded?" Rae said, draping an arm over Mandy's shoulder.

"Man, do you realize where we just came from? Your place sounds like a mansion."

"It is, but we want everyone to have their own space and comfort."

Rae gave him the side-eye. "Be honest, you don't want to be around a bunch of ex cons."

One side of Chaz's mouth tipped in a smile. "False."

Nikki tilted her head and looked at the other women. "What?"

"You are not ex-cons," he countered. "Your records were expunged before we left the country. That still sticks."

"Still doesn't make us less in your eyes if you're thinking that way," she said, giving him a sly grin.

Chaz replied, "My wife vouched for each one of you and I trust her judgement. If I felt different, I would have left every single one of you in Mississippi to go your way."

"My bad." Rae gave him a sheepish smile. "Just a little sensitive here, that's all."

Chaz returned her smile. "No problem, given the circumstances," he countered.

"It'll be just like old times." Linda laid her head on Mandy's shoulder.

"My God, I hope not," Mandy said. "Climbing onto the top bunk was hell."

Rae embraced Mandy then pulled Chaz in for a group hug. "Thank you."

"I couldn't leave y'all in there," Mandy whispered. "I just couldn't. Not if I had the means to bring you out."

The lavish space featured light oak flooring and cream furniture with gold accents and pops of blues.

"This is the guest room," Nita and Karen said, then gestured to an area down the hall from the master suite. "We'll have the nursery suite—three bedrooms—converted for our guests."

"No, put us all in here," Rae said, nodding to the guest room. "We're not displacing your babies."

"They aren't going to know the difference," Chaz said, frowning.

"It's only temporary," Mandy said and Rae pulled her in to embrace her again.

"Hey, you keep that up and I'm going to think she wanted you out for entirely different reasons," Chaz taunted.

"Down, cowboy," Rae teased. "All she could talk about is you. Teaching us yoga and meditation and stuff. Trust me, she is strictly about the peen, not the peach."

Everyone laughed and Chaz's lips turned up at the corners as he shook his head.

Before Mandy could slide a word in edgewise, Karen slid up and put her arms about Mandy's shoulders and said, "Soneni said lunch will be served in about ten minutes. Then you ladies can go shopping, and to a spa."

"Spa?" Linda said with a playful sigh and hands dramatically over her heart. "I have died and gone to Heaven."

"Do you think we can phone home?" Nikki said on a hopeful note.

"They're working on it so you'll have a secure line," Chaz said.

Rae squeezed Mandy's hand hard. "Why am I so afraid? This is freedom, right?"

"It's all right," Mandy answered, placing a hand over Rae's heart. "We'll get through it together."

Chapter 30

Three months later, when the house was settled into silence, Chaz lay next to Mandy in their bedroom with a view of the towering landscape of the downtown Durabia skyline. He was getting used to the changes in her since that short stint in a place she called "the pokey". The small amount of time seemed an eternity on his end, but had made a world of difference for the women who were now living in a condo a few blocks from them. They visited so often, they might as well have kept their spot in his home. He didn't mind it so much. Especially given the fact that the women brought just as much joy and laughter as their children, and their staff who were now considered family. Well, he would have to add himself as well. Not because he wanted it to be so, but because Mandy said it all the time. "I never knew joy, love, and peace until I met you."

The women, who were now in yoga and meditation with him and Mandy on the mornings they arrived near breakfast time, were putting their heads together to do big things, great things. The more Mandy focused on founding an organization that would help so many others, the less time she had to entertain her sorrows and anger, which were subsiding by the day. The moment that Mandy realized her true purpose, was when Sharla, the last inmate on their cell block was released from prison. Every single woman that was with them during that time, had effected a change that started from the inside and transformed their world.

"That's why I had to go in," she said one day over dinner. "I had to shake off that part of my life. I had to release my guilt, my pain—all of it. I left one house of sorrows, but I was still stuck and chained to another one. Confronted my worst fears." She glanced out to the women at the table and said. "I went in for you. I went in because it was the only way to shine a light on the horrors that were being committed in the name of justice."

Chaz understood every aspect of that. And he would do everything in his power to support her in this, and any, endeavor.

He was still teasing them about the fact that on their first day of arrival, the spa called him in to retrieve Mandy and the women because they all fell asleep on the massage table and no one could wake them up. He had to shell out a great deal of extra cash for the staff to remain, allowing the women to awaken at their leisure. To him, it was money well spent.

Then to make matters even more wonderful, Khalil had come to Durabia to welcome them all home. Because of their work with the women in both American and Durabia, and Chaz's efforts in the area in which he was raised, Khalil had given him an equity stake in The Castle, as the Knight of Bronzeville. Chaz had gladly accepted his place among those powerful men and vowed to live up to their humanitarian expectations.

"Too excited that we're together again," he whispered.

A gentle smile lifted her lips. "Not as happy as I am."

"Woman, I missed you so much, I can't even explain."

"Trust me, I have an idea. At first, torture couldn't describe what it was like being in that place. The only things that kept me sane were thoughts of you and our children. Remembering those words you wrote about me on the island, before you even knew you loved me. And then, when they asked me to teach them what I learned from you, it made things so much better."

Chaz felt all kinds of warm behind that admission. "I'm glad you finally accepted how you feel about me." He moved his hand back and forth between them. "About us."

She sighed and turned into his embrace in the circular king-size bed. "Oh, yes."

Their lips met in a searing kiss that reminded him of everything he'd been longing for during her time away. After exchanging several more kisses, he trailed his lips down her neck and separated the folds of her robe to drink in the beauty laid before him under the muted light coming from the open window. Her body's response to the cool air flowing across her breasts thrilled him.

He lowered his head and teased that little bud of arousal before his tongue secured it tightly within the warmth of his lips. An unexpected trickle of liquid filled his mouth and he paused, processing what had transpired.

Mandy tensed, her eyes opened and locked in on him as he let the sweetness slide down his throat.

"What's wrong?"

"Nothing," he said, realizing that she wasn't aware of what had happened, and he wasn't willing to give her false hope. She cried sometimes because she was unable to nurse their children. The time spent away from them had cost her in more ways than one. "Close your eyes."

She complied and he switched his effort to her other breast, watching to see if she noticed the change in her body.

Mandy didn't, and he believed that her arousal had relaxed her body enough for the milk to express. After ensuring that the flow had started, he eased inside her, joining them completely. Her gasps and moans of pleasure confirmed she was enjoying their loving-making; their connection, as much as he.

Chaz brushed his fingertips across those engorged nipples, relishing her sharp intake of breath. The way her body trembled in response to his touch filled him with such joy. Each circular motion of his hips was answered with an equally slow counterclockwise circuit and thrust of her own, pushing him deeper and deeper within her, removing the last measure of distance between them. Her tongue flicked against the place just below his left ear before she lined his collar bone with kisses.

Every passion-soaked plea, every sigh she breathed, stoked a deeper fire beneath his skin.

The feel of her, the rich wonderful scent of her bombarded his senses. He was lost *in* her … lost *to* her, and he desired nothing more. The signs of their union fused them mind, body, and soul. If hereafter existed, he didn't care. All he had … all he ever needed was right there in his arms.

As she slipped an arm around his neck to draw him closer, she moaned his name. "Come for me, Chaz. Come inside me."

The heat exploded around him and he remained still, savoring the connection for several moments, then moving, creating a rhythm that only crooners The Isley Brothers, Charlie Wilson, and Luther Vandross made sure everyone understood.

When they were finally sated, Mandy closed her eyes and surrendered to sleep.

Chaz drew the sheets around them and watched her, guarding their union from the world with his heart full and his body wanting more.

A lifetime of more.

* * *

Mandy nursed one of the triplets, sitting in the rocking chair on the penthouse's balcony. Rae, Linda, and Nikki had situated themselves nearby, around the patio table. They were discussing plans for a place in Durabia and in the States to help women with a past—some from the place they left a few months ago; those who wanted a second chance at life; those who had been framed and railroaded by the same system that had done so many injustices to other women.

"We need transitional housing for them until they find their way," Rae announced, pulling her gaze from the street below.

Linda's head shot up from her papers. "I thought we were getting them permanent housing while they do skills training or search for a job."

"I don't want them to be like the Nigerians, Indians, and Pakistanis over here." Mandy had seen a news report on African people coming over for job sharing and living in a space with up to eight people or more while looking for employment. They congregated in one community within Durabia, hustling for an opportunity before being forced to return to their homeland.

Rae sipped her lemonade. "I'm not suggesting that. However, it would be better to set up permanent housing later but it's based on whatever income we're able to get for them."

"She has a point. We don't want to set them up for failure," Nikki chimed in.

"Let's get all our ideas out," Mandy said, gently rocking baby Tara in her arms as Malik and Saira rested in the arms of Rae and Nita. "Then as we learn more about what programs are already available in Durabia and study rehabilitation programs that have high success rates, we'll know which direction to take."

The goal was to have the ladies run all of the rehabilitation centers.

Linda would handle intake. Rae, once she made the trip home to Shadow Bay to settle matters with her family, would be responsible for training. Nikki would be in charge of placement. Sabrina ... well, she was still tucked away in The Castle because she feared what would happen if she left. No matter how many times Shaz or Vikkas explained that she was free and no chance of being carted back off to Mississippi existed, Sabrina didn't believe them. Mandy and Chaz were going to make a visit with the crew—as Mandy called them—to pluck her from the tower of the castle and bring her, and her family, to their new place in Durabia.

"We'll revisit our list, finalize the plan," Mandy said. "Then present our ideas to Sheikh Kamran and Sheikha Ellena."

"I'm good with that," Rae said as Nikki and Linda nodded.

Chaz stepped out onto the balcony. First, he kissed Tara's forehead then Mandy's. Their oldest daughter reached for him and he happily obliged. "Ladies, dinner is ready."

Nita took the baby from Rae, while Karen stepped out and scooped up Malik who was fast becoming a charmer. The ladies gathered the papers from the patio table and headed inside.

As Mandy stood and moved toward the door, Chaz gently clasped her arm, bringing her to a halt. "How did the meeting go?"

"It went great," she replied. "I'm so happy that my friends are adjusting so well."

"I am glad." He nuzzled her neck. "Let's go celebrate your new venture and the ladies getting their own places."

Their condos were on the last phases of the remodel efforts. Each had picked a décor that fit their personalities to a "T".

Her goal was to get the rehabilitation program up and running in Durabia then duplicate it in the States. The plan needed to be established since Sabrina was now cleared by the authorities. If she didn't want to bring her family to the Middle East, she'd at least have a job. Sabrina could run the program state side. Not bad for women who were devoid of hope a short time ago.

Mandy smiled. Life was surprisingly good. She couldn't lie, being this happy frightened her. Chaz grabbed her hand and led her to the long oak dining table filled with people she'd grown to love. Sheikh Kamran and Sheikha Ellena were there. She still was so amazed at having to call her sister by that title. The unfortunate circumstances surrounding Sheikh Kamran's sudden ascension to the throne had the countries surrounding Durabia up in arms and gunning for Sheikha Ellena. A bounty had been placed on her life because of what she had done to escape the Sheikh of Nadaum who had kidnapped her the moment Kamran was considered a threat for ascension to the throne. The punishments given to Sheikh Kamran's family for their part in things, in Mandy's estimation, were far too kind.

Soon, Christian would be back in Durabia as well, then Blair. The family members who actually had some common sense would surround her. With all the drama she'd been through, her other sisters and her brother could stay their behinds right there in Chicago. Except Melissa. They would have to find a way to bring her as well.

Chaz sat up, his shoulders tense as he glanced at his phone and said, "Whoa."

"Chaz?"

"No, it's nothing," he said, closing his screen and placing the phone in his pocket.

"No secrets," she protested as all other conversation at the table came to a halt. "We said no secrets between us. No matter how hard the truth might hit."

Chaz scanned the expectant faces a moment before saying, "Susan's been indicted."

Mandy held out her hand. "Let me see that."

He obliged, placing the phone in her hand even though the grimace said he was still reluctant to share more than he already had. "Evidently, one of the reasons she was trying to hold onto the properties that were in my name, is that she knew the rest of her assets were going to the family of a man she caused irreparable harm at the request of one of the judge's business associates. There's been a pattern of such thing and the medical board was in the process of revoking her license when she was released on bail. She fled the country before her trial."

"That's not good," Rae said, frowning. "Especially if she landed in a place that doesn't have an extradition treaty with America."

"This made international news," Chaz said. "They'll find her. Eventually."

Mandy sighed. "We can only hope."

After dinner, she put the babies to bed, then Mandy finally had the time to reflect on all the wonderful things that came from that fated trip to Jamaica. Until this point, her life had been nothing but pain and shadows. She had been through so much and didn't think it would ever change until she met Chaz.

He, and the possibilities of everything that they now stood for, gave her life new meaning and understanding.

She walked the hallway of her dream home until she made it into their master bedroom suite. Mandy closed the door behind her and joined him in bed. Though sleeping, his arms instinctively reached out to gather her to his body. She settled into a familiar feel—comfort, love, safety … peace.

Who knew she would find the man of her dreams, become a mother to not one, but three children, and gain a whole new family? Mandy was ready to take on life with open arms. For the first time, she was looking forward to her future.

Her happily ever after.

About the *Knights of the Castle* Series

Don't miss the hot new standalone series. The Kings of the Castle made them family, but the Knights will transform the world.

Book 1 - King of Durabia – Naleighna Kai

No good deed goes unpunished, or that's how Ellena Kiley feels after she rescues a child and the former Crown Prince of Durabia offers to marry her.

Kamran learns of a nefarious plot to undermine his position with the Sheikh and jeopardize his ascent to the throne. He's unsure how Ellena, the fiery American seductress, fits into the plan but she's a secret weapon he's unwilling to relinquish.

Ellena is considered a sister by the Kings of the Castle and her connection to Kamran challenges her ideals, her freedoms, and her heart. Plus, loving him makes her a potential target for his enemies. When Ellena is kidnapped, Kamran is forced to bring in the Kings.

In the race against time to rescue his woman and defeat his enemies, the kingdom of Durabia will never be the same.

Book 2 - Knight of Bronzeville – Naleighna Kai and Stephanie M. Freeman

Chaz Maharaj thought he could maintain the lie of a perfect marriage for his adoring fans … until he met Amanda.

The connection between them should have ended with that unconditional "hall pass" which led to one night of unbridled passion. But once would never satisfy his hunger for a woman who could never be his. When Amanda walked out of his life, it was supposed to be forever. Neither of them could have anticipated fate's plan.

Chaz wants to explore his feelings for Amanda, but Susan has other ideas. Prepared to fight for his budding romance and navigate a plot that's been laid to crush them, an unexpected twist threatens his love and her life.

When Amanda's past comes back to haunt them, Chaz enlists the Kings of the Castle to save his newfound love in a daring escape.

Book 3 - Knight of South Holland – Karen D. Bradley

He's a brilliant inventor, but he'll decimate anyone who threatens his woman.

When the Kings of the Castle recommend Calvin Atwood, strategic defense inventor, to create a security shield for the kingdom of Durabia, it's the opportunity of a lifetime. The only problem—it's a two-year assignment and he promised his fiancée they would step away from their dangerous lifestyle and start a family.

Security specialist, Mia Jakob, adores Calvin with all her heart, but his last assignment put both of their lives at risk. She understands how important this new role is to the man she loves, but the thought that he may be avoiding commitment does cross her mind.

Calvin was sure he'd made the best decision for his and Mia's future, until enemies of the state target his invention and his woman. Set on a collision course with hidden foes, this Knight will need the help of the Kings to save both his Queen and the Kingdom of Durabia.

Book 4 - Lady of Jeffrey Manor – J. S. Cole and Naleighna Kai

He's the kingdom's most eligible bachelor. She's a practical woman on temporary assignment.

When surgical nurse, Blair Swanson, departed the American Midwest for an assignment in the Kingdom of Durabia she had no intention of finding love.

As a member of the royal family, Crown Prince Hassan has a responsibility to the throne. A loveless, arranged marriage is his duty, but the courageous American nurse is his desire.

When a dark secret threatens everything Hassan holds dear, how will he fulfill his royal duty and save the lady who holds his heart?

Book 5 - Knight of Grand Crossing – Hiram Shogun Harris, Naleighna Kai, and Anita L. Roseboro

Rahm did time for a crime he didn't commit. Now that he's free, taking care of the three women who supported him on a hellish journey is his priority, but old enemies are waiting in the shadows.

Rahm Fosten's dream life as a Knight of the Castle includes Marilyn Spears, who quiets the injustice of his rough past, but in his absence a new foe has infiltrated his family.

Marilyn Spears waited for many years to have someone like Rahm in her life. Now that he's home, an unexpected twist threatens to rip him away again. As much as she loves him, she's not willing to go where this new drama may lead.

Meanwhile, Rahm's gift to his Aunt Alyssa brings her to Durabia, where she catches the attention of wealthy surgeon, Ahmad Maharaj. Her attendance at a private Bliss event puts her under his watchful eye, but also in the crosshairs of the worst kind of enemy. Definitely the wrong timing for the rest of the challenges Rahm is facing.

While Rahm and Marilyn navigate their romance, a deadly threat has him and the Kings of the Castle primed to keep Marilyn, Alyssa, and his family from falling prey to an adversary out for bloody revenge.

Book 6 - Knight of Paradise Island – J. L. Campbell

Someone is killing women and the villain's next target strikes too close to the Kingdom of Durabia.

Dorian "Ryan" Bostwick is a protector and he's one of the best in the business. When a King of the Castle assigns him to find his former lover, Aziza, he stumbles upon a deadly underworld operating close to the Durabian border.

Aziza Hampton had just rekindled her love affair with Ryan when a night out with friends ends in her kidnapping. Alone and scared, she must find a way to escape her captor and reunite with her lover.

In a race against time, Ryan and the Kings of the Castle follow ominous clues into the underbelly of a system designed to take advantage of the vulnerable. Failure isn't an option and Ryan will rain down hell on earth to save the woman of his heart.

Book 7 - Knight of Irondale – J. L Woodson, Naleighna Kai, and Martha Kennerson

Neesha Carpenter is on the run from a stalker ex-boyfriend, so why are the police hot on her trail?

Neesha escaped the madness of her previous relationship only to discover the Chicago Police have named her the prime suspect in her ex's shooting. With her life spinning out of control, she turns to the one man who's the biggest threat to her heart—Christian Vidal, her high school sweetheart.

Christian has always been smitten with Neesha's strength, intelligence and beauty. He offers her safe haven in the kingdom of Durabia and will do whatever it takes to keep her safe, even enlisting the help of the Kings of the Castle.

Neesha and Christian's rekindled flame burns hotter even as her stay in the country places the royal family at odds with the American government.

As mounting evidence points to Neesha's guilt, Christian must ask the hard question … is the woman he loves being framed or did she pull the trigger?

Book 8 - Knight of Birmingham – Lori Hays and MarZe Scott

Single mothers who are eligible for release, have totally disappeared from the Alabama justice system.

Women's advocate, Meghan Turner, has uncovered a disturbing pattern and she's desperate for help. Then her worse nightmare becomes a horrific reality when her friend goes missing under the same mysterious circumstances.

Rory Tannous has spent his life helping society's most vulnerable. When he learns of Meghan's dilemma, he takes it personal. Rory has his own tragic past and he'll utilize every connection, even the King of the Castle, to help this intriguing woman find her friend and the other women.

As Rory and Meghan work together, the attraction grows and so does the danger. The stakes are high and they will have to risk their love and lives to defeat a powerful adversary.

Book 9 - Knight of Penn Quarter – Terri Ann Johnson and Michele Sims

Following an undercover FBI sting operation that didn't go as planned, Agent Mateo Lopez is ready to put the government agency in his rearview mirror.

A confirmed workaholic, his career soared at the cost of his love life which had crashed and burned until mutual friends arranged a date with beautiful, sharp-witted, Rachel Jordan, a rising star at a children's social services agency.

Unlucky in love, Rachel has sworn off romantic relationships, but Mateo finds himself falling for her in more ways than one. When trouble brews in one of Rachel's cases, he does everything in his power to keep her safe—even if it means resorting to extreme measures.

Will the choices they make bring them closer together or cost them their lives?

About the Kings of the Castle Series

"Did you miss The Kings of the Castle? "They are so expertly crafted and flow so well between each of the books, it's hard to tell each is crafted by a different author. Very well done!" - Lori H..., Amazon and Goodreads

Each King book 2-9 is a standalone, NO cliffhangers

Book 1 – Kings of the Castle, the introduction to the series and story of King of Wilmette (Vikkas Germaine)

USA TODAY, *New York Times,* and National Bestselling Authors work together to provide you with a world you'll never want to leave. The Castle.

Fate made them brothers, but protecting the Castle, each other, and the women they love, will make them Kings. Their combined efforts to find the current Castle members responsible for the attempt on their mentor's life, is the beginning of dangerous challenges that will alter the path of their lives forever.

These powerful men, unexpectedly brought together by their pasts and current circumstances, will become a force to be reckoned with.

King of Chatham - Book 2 – London St. Charles

While Mariano "Reno" DeLuca uses his skills and resources to create safe havens for battered women, a surge in criminal activity within the Chatham area threatens the women's anonymity and security. When Zuri, an exotic Tanzanian Princess, arrives seeking refuge from an arranged marriage and its deadly consequences, Reno is now forced to relocate the women in the shelter, fend off unforeseen enemies of The Castle, and endeavor not to lose his heart to the mysterious woman.

King of Evanston - Book 3 - J. L. Campbell

Raised as an immigrant, he knows the heartache of family separation firsthand. His personal goals and business ethics collide when a vulnerable woman stands to lose her baby in an underhanded and profitable scheme crafted by powerful, ruthless businessmen and politicians who have nefarious ties to The Castle. Shaz and the Kings of the Castle collaborate to uproot the dark forces intent on changing the balance of power within The Castle and destroying their mentor. National Bestselling Author, J.L. Campbell presents book 3 in the Kings of the Castle Series, featuring Shaz Bostwick.

King of Devon - Book 4 - Naleighna Kai

When a coma patient becomes pregnant, Jaidev Maharaj's medical facility comes under a government microscope and media scrutiny. In the midst of the investigation, he receives a mysterious call from someone in his past that demands that more of him than he's ever been willing to give and is made aware of a dark family secret that will destroy the people he loves most.

King of Morgan Park - Book 5 - Karen D. Bradley

Two things threaten to destroy several areas of Daron Kincaid's life—the tracking device he developed to locate victims of sex trafficking and an inherited membership in a mysterious outfit called The Castle. The new developments set the stage to dismantle the relationship with a woman who's been trained to make men weak or put them on the other side of the grave. The secrets Daron keeps from Cameron and his inner circle only complicates an already tumultuous situation caused by an FBI sting that brought down his former enemies. Can Daron take on his enemies, manage his secrets and loyalty to the Castle without permanently losing the woman he loves?

King of South Shore - Book 6 - MarZe Scott

Award-winning real estate developer, Kaleb Valentine, is known for turning failing communities into thriving havens in the Metro Detroit area. His plans to rebuild his hometown neighborhood are derailed with one phone call that puts Kaleb deep in the middle of an intense criminal investigation led by a detective who has a personal vendetta. Now he will have to deal with the ghosts of his past before they kill him.

King of Lincoln Park - Book 7 – Martha Kennerson

Grant Khambrel is a sexy, successful architect with big plans to expand his Texas Company. Unfortunately, a dark secret from his past could destroy it all unless he's willing to betray the man responsible for that success, and the woman who becomes the key to his salvation.

King of Hyde Park - Book 8 -Lisa Dodson

Alejandro "Dro" Reyes has been a "fixer" for as long as he could remember, which makes owning a crisis management company focused on repairing professional reputations the perfect fit. The same could be said of Lola Samuels, who is only vaguely aware of his "true" talents and seems to be oblivious to the growing attraction between them. His company, Vantage Point, is in high demand and business in the Windy City is booming. Until a mysterious call following an attempt on his mentor's life forces him to drop everything and accept a fated position with The Castle. But there's a hidden agenda and unexpected enemy that Alejandro doesn't see coming who threatens his life, his woman, and his throne.

King of Lawndale - Book 9 - Janice M. Allen

Dwayne Harper's passion is giving disadvantaged boys the tools to transform themselves into successful men. Unfortunately, the minute he steps up to take his place among the men he considers brothers, two things stand in his way: a political office that does not want the competition Dwayne's new education system will bring, and a well-connected former member of The Castle who will use everything in his power—even those who Dwayne mentors—to shut him down.

Naleighna Kai is the *USA TODAY*, *Essence®*, and national bestselling and award-winning author of several women's fiction, contemporary fiction, Christian fiction, Romance, erotica, and science fiction novels that plumb the depth of unique relationships and women's issues. She is also a contributor to a New York Times bestseller, one of AALBC's 100 Top Authors, a member of CVS Hall of Fame, Mercedes Benz Mentor Award Nominee, and the E. Lynn Harris Author of Distinction. In addition to successfully cracking the code of landing a deal for herself and others with a major publishing house, she continues to "pay it forward" by organizing the annual Cavalcade of Authors and NK Tribe Called Success which offers aspiring and established authors assistance with ghostwriting, developmental editing, publishing, marketing, and other services to jump-start or enhance their writing careers.

www.naleighnakai.com

Stephanie M. Freeman is a preeminent author whose professional writing career began in 2012 when her first, *Thriller, Necessary Evil*, followed by *Unfinished Business* and *Nature of the Beast* were released. Since then, she has explored different genres and amassed a loyal group of fans who eagerly await her latest releases. She continues to push literary boundaries and also writes lighter themes under Aracyne Kelly and more sensual pleasures under Red Widow.

Stephanie is surrounded by an eclectic group of friends and family she affectionately calls "The Usual Suspects". Although she spent her formative years in Maryland, she is a proud Pennsylvanian where she shares her book lair and a seemingly endless array of crochet projects with her horribly spoiled cat, Egypt. She is currently working on *Season of the Blood*, the fourth installment of the Diamonds, Blood, and Shadows series. www.stephaniemfreemanauthor.com